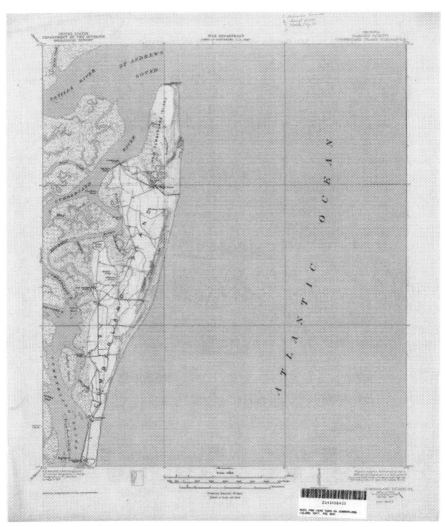

Courtesy of the University of Texas Libraries, The University of Texas at Austin.

Master Robert

ROBERT L. STEVENS

authorHOUSE®

AuthorHouse™
1663 Liberty Drive
Bloomington, IN 47403
www.authorhouse.com
Phone: 1 (800) 839-8640

Biblical quotations taken from the King James Version of the Holy
Bible (Wheaton, IL: Tyndale Publishers, 1979).

Published by AuthorHouse   04/24/2017

ISBN: 978-1-5246-8969-8 (sc)
ISBN: 978-1-5246-8970-4 (hc)
ISBN: 978-1-5246-8971-1 (e)

Library of Congress Control Number: 2017906306

Print information available on the last page.

For Chelsea

1

Hurricane

High in the sky, wisps of white clouds like filaments scud toward Amos and Amelia as they leave the slave quarters and walk slowly toward the salt marsh. A large reed basket gently rocks between them. They walk past Tom, their best friend, who is hoeing turnip greens. He sees them and yells over the fence, "Where are you going?"

"Down to the salt marsh to pull some oysters. Want to come?" Amos replies.

"Be right with you." Tom leans his hoe against the fence. "This will be more fun than weeding turnips."

They usually fish for the large stone crabs or blue crabs. Both are delicacies, but today they will pull oysters. Blue crabs share the same marsh creeks where large quantities of eastern oysters tenaciously cling to the mud banks. When the tidal estuaries empty the marsh, beds of gray oysters lie waiting to be harvested.

The air is heavy. Trees framing the road stand mute. Leaves hang listlessly. The only breeze that stirs the air comes from the movement of a monarch butterfly seeking moisture from a leaf.

For the past several weeks, rain and heat have visited the island in monotonous regularity. The ground is swollen with water, and the low-lying sloughs are full. The brilliant sun evaporates the surface moisture. It condenses and forms popcorn clouds that bring showers late in the day. The cycle of heat, humidity, and rain continues.

The marsh is home to cordgrass. Periwinkles attach themselves to the long, broad leaf blades. Salt grass and pickleweed, succulent plants with tiny leaves, grow in the high marsh a few steps away. Tidal creeks meander through the marsh and then run into Cumberland Sound. The tide is running out as Amos, Amelia, and Tom cross the marsh flats. Black ooze, full of detritus, squishes between their toes and tickles them. The smell of decayed animal, fish, and plant life permeates their nostrils.

"Boy, this marsh stinks," Tom blurts out.

"It's this terrible heat that's causing the smell," Amelia says.

"Let's get into the water, pull some oysters, and cool off," Amos says.

When they arrive at the estuary that splits the marsh in two, Amos instructs Tom to get into the water with the oyster beds and tells Amelia to stay up on the marsh grass with the basket. "We will toss the oysters up to you, and you put them in the basket," Amos says.

Tom and Amos stand ankle-deep in the water. They pluck the oysters that are clinging tenaciously to the rocks and toss them to Amelia. Families of brown pelicans coming in off the ocean fly over their heads. Amos looks up as they pass. He hasn't noticed the sky before.

"Those are strange-looking clouds," Amos says to Amelia. "I have never seen any like that before."

"They're so high in the sky … they look like horses' tails," Amelia replies.

"Most clouds are white and puffy, fair-weather clouds," Amos says.

"Yeah, but the low and gray clouds bring rain," Tom replies.

Amelia gazes steadily at the clouds. "But these are different," she says. "They are much higher in the sky. I wonder what they will bring."

Clouds of war are also forming over Washington City and Richmond, Virginia. Two presidents, Abraham Lincoln and Jefferson Davis, order their generals to prepare for what will be the first battle of the Civil War. Union troops will march from Washington City to attack Confederate defenders at Manassas Junction, a strategic rail line in northern Virginia. For the next four years, the country will be at war.

When the oyster basket is full to the rim, the three trudge back across the marsh. They are excited about the number of oysters they have harvested. The heat is sweltering. Beads of sweat gently roll off their foreheads and run down their arms. Rivulets of mud make their arms and legs sticky. Suddenly, they hear a wave crash on the beach and then another. When they are pulling oysters in the stream bed, they cannot hear the ocean. For a moment, they freeze. Crashing waves? But the air is still; there is no wind.

Tom helps Amos carry the full basket. "Something doesn't feel right," he says.

Amos, usually skeptical when Tom seems out of sorts, has the same ominous feeling. "Let's run to the top of the dunes and see what is going on," he says.

Dropping the basket of oysters, the three race across the marsh and climb to the top of the nearest sand dune. The sand scorches their feet. "Boy, this is hot," Tom says.

Two things catch their attention as they scan the ocean: long, undulating waves crashing on the beach and a strange, hazy, copper glow appearing on the horizon.

"Those waves are strange," Tom says. "Look! No white caps. There is no wind pushing them."

"And the sky is a strange color too," Amelia says.

"Let's get these oysters home as soon as possible. Something strange is going on."

Amos, Amelia, and Tom are survivors of tropical storms, drenching rains, thunderstorms that crackle with lightning strikes, and gusty squalls associated with rapidly moving frontal systems. They, like all the residents of Cumberland Island, have adapted to the rhythms of the weather. But they never have experienced a hurricane. That is about to change.

———⟨⟩———

Tucked in close to the Georgia and Florida coasts, Cumberland Island is uniquely situated to avoid most major Atlantic storms. The warm waters of the Gulf Stream flow away from the island in a northeasterly direction. Most of the time, destructive hurricanes make landfall further up the coast in Charleston, South Carolina, or the Outer Banks. It is rare for a hurricane to bring its destructive winds and storm surges onto Cumberland Island.

Before the advent of weather forecasting, hurricanes wrought destruction and hardship because they were unpredictable. No one knows how many hurricanes were spawned in the eighteenth and nineteenth centuries; historians know only the ones that made landfall or were recorded in ships' logs that survived crossing the Atlantic Ocean. Of course, Amos, Amelia, and Tom know none of this. In fact, they know nothing about hurricanes.

Far to the east, on the African continent, hurricanes breed. A prolonged drought in the Western Sahel may account for hurricanes on the East Coast of the United States. Rising heat from the 113-degree temperature soars in large thermals, rapidly rising hot air to altitudes exceeding four miles. Particles of dust and sand rise into the atmosphere from a fierce, hot, easterly wind blowing out over the cool and moist bulge of Africa; they set in motion eddies of air that soon became small cyclones. A storm may originate from a single molecule ascending into the atmosphere. The gasses associated with decaying vegetation, animal dung, and human fires gently drift and finally are pushed by the ascending mix of air, forming a devil's cauldron, a brew so toxic and potent it splinters the largest of ships and the tallest of buildings into shreds.

In West Africa, long lines of slaves sold by African chieftains to white slavers march to waiting ships. The dry wind blows the dust they and their animals kick up high into the air. Great clouds of dust follow these caravans of slaves to their unknown destinies. The ships that house them in holds—packed together and chained to decks—sail along the same ocean currents that serve as conduits for the deadly hurricanes. Like leaves carried along a stream, both slave ships and hurricanes will reach the ports of the eastern United States.

Dust particles driven by the easterly flow collide with moist air that comes from the Atlantic. This convergence produces instability in the upper atmosphere and creates embryonic eddies. Though most dissipate, a few become destructive storms.

The heat produced by winds blowing over the water causes large amounts of condensation to form. A storm's primary source of energy is the released heat condensing from water vapor at very high altitudes. Much of the released energy drives updrafts that increase the height of storm clouds, which in turn, speeds up condensation. This is called a positive feedback loop and, once it forms, a tropical storm develops. Trade winds steer tropical waves westward from Africa toward the Caribbean Sea and the East Coast of the United States. In the nineteenth century, except for crews on ships far out into the Atlantic, no one is aware of the development or movement of these storms. The ability to predict hurricanes, the most devastating of all storms, does not yet exist.

"Let's get back and tell Mr. Robert what we have just seen," says Amos.

He and Tom race back to the basket of oysters with Amelia. She runs ahead. The boys each grab a handle and head off the marsh toward the maritime forest and Planter's House. The sun is high in the sky, the heat is unbearable, and not a leaf stirs. It is as if a vacuum has sucked all the energy from the island.

The walk back to Planter's House and the slave quarters is arduous. Though delighted with the size of their oyster harvest, they feel the basket grow heavier with each step. Both Tom and Amos drip with sweat.

"Let's stop and rest," Tom pleads.

"Not a bad idea," Amos says.

Even in the shade of the maritime forest, they still feel the heat of the sun. Their breathing is labored.

"I feel like someone just walked over my chest," Tom says.

Amelia takes this opportunity to taunt them. "Can't you two carry a few oysters?" Slowly they make their way. Finally, Amelia yells, "I can see the wall! We are almost there."

Tom and Amos carry the basket into the slave quarters. They sit down and rest in front of Old Jake's cabin. Old Jake hears them, opens the door, sees the basket, and says, "Now there's a mighty mess of oysters."

"Mr. Jake." Amelia is the first to speak. "The sky at the beach is funny-looking, and we saw large waves rolling onto the beach, but there was no wind."

Jake straightens and grits his teeth. His gray eyebrows furrow. He looks into the distance as if he's trying to remember something.

"Tell me that again," he said.

Amelia repeats what she's just said.

"You better go and tell Master Robert that we are in for a big blow," Old Jake says. "When I was your age, we suffered a mighty storm. It destroyed our crops, flooded most of the island, and blew the roof off General Greene's mansion. I can feel it in the air. My bones are acting up. This hot spell without a breath of air is a sign of things to come. Terrible things, I am afraid."

"What kinds of terrible things?" they all ask.

"We don't have time to talk … Just go and warn Master Robert," Jake says firmly.

They race to Planter's House. The sky is overcast, and an eerie glow falls over the forest like a gossamer sheet. All three bound onto the veranda and rap on the front door.

'Mr. James! Mr. James!" they yell together. "Where's Master Robert?"

"Calm down, you young ones … what's got you so spooked, did you see a haint in the forest?"

"No, but maybe worse than a haint—a big storm is coming."

The commotion on the veranda attracts Master Robert's attention. He is in his study reading a contract. He puts it down on his desk and walks slowly toward the front of the house.

"What's all this noise about?" he asks.

Amos, Amelia, and Tom repeat their observations.

"You saw long rolling waves crash on the beach? Why, there hasn't been any wind for days," he says. "Tell me again about the color of the sky."

Master Robert's face looks very serious. Amos wonders what he is thinking.

"Amos, get my buggy. You and I are going down to the beach."

Amos pulls the buggy to the front of Planter's House as he is instructed. Master Robert climbs onto the seat.

"Let's go!"

The air is heavier than before. The weight presses on both Master Robert and Amos, who tries to make sense of Old Jake's reaction and Mr. Robert's concern. He feels that something is wrong but can't figure out what. Mr. Robert seldom tells him to drive the buggy to the beach; usually he drives the master to a cotton field, to a timber stand on the north end, or down to the dock to get the mail. The tackie pulling the buggy whinnies and balks a few times, which adds to the mystery.

They emerge from the maritime forest. To the right lies the marsh where Amos pulls oysters, and straight ahead, the beach awaits. The sun struggles to shine thorough the haze that covers it. Master Robert has an excellent view of the ocean and the horizon from his high perch on the buggy. A large wave crashes onto the beach, rolls over the baby dunes, and spews frothy foam into the interdune meadow. When the wave recedes and races back into the sea, the small dunes are washed out to sea. *The tide will not be high for another four hours*, Mr. Robert thinks to himself. He grows more anxious.

"You were right to warn us about what you saw this morning," he tells Amos. "Out there, somewhere, there is a big storm. See the waves undulate? That means a force is pushing them to our island. Look at the sky."

It is a brilliant mother-of-pearl with shades of copper, reds, and yellows dancing about. "The last time I saw a sky like this," Master Robert says, "I was your age, and a terrible storm swept over us. Let's get back and warn the others. We have lots to do."

By the time Master Robert and Amos return to Planter's House, the alarm has spread into the slave community and to all parts of the island. The line of communication among slaves is a long-established one, and soon everyone knows. Slaves who cut timber at Table Point on the north end leave their axes and march down the main road toward Planter's House. The field slaves cultivating cotton on the Rayfield tract also return to Planter's House. Soon the slave quarters are humming like a bees' nest with the news of the impending storm. The older slaves and Master Robert survived a major hurricane that demolished many parts of the island in 1813. Though a major storm of that magnitude has not visited the island since then, their collective memories will aid the survival of the throngs of slaves gathering close to Planter's House.

Many of the older slaves are fearful. Memories of losing family members when they were children surface, as, for the very first time in days, wind ripples through the leaves and turns them over, showing their silvery undersides. They have not forgotten the terror they experienced when their homes were demolished when large trees uprooted and fell over. Several slaves were crushed under the enormous weight of trees. They know they will not be safe. Agitated, they speak sharply to the younger ones, particularly the children.

"Get to high ground and stay away from trees," they yell into the wind. "When the water rises, snakes will slither up the trees and bite anyone close by."

Amos skillfully handles the buggy as it comes to a halt in front of the house. Mr. Robert jumps from the buggy to the veranda. "Amos, ring the alarm bell!" he shouts.

Amos grabs a forged metal rod and rings the triangular-shaped bell. He beats it as hard as he can. Slaves close by cup their hands over their ears. The noise is deafening.

"You overseers, come quick," Mr. Robert yells.

They quickly gather in front of the veranda.

"Arabella! Where's Arabella?" he asks.

"In the hospital!" someone cries.

"Go! Get her," he orders. "Tom, Dido, Phineas, separate everyone into groups, each one with an equal number of people. Make sure that someone watches the children. If they get scared they might run."

Mr. Robert owns 350 slaves, all of whom desperately need protection from the coming hurricane. He remembers the 1813 storm, which caught the island by surprise; many slaves drowned as they tried to reach higher ground.

Planter's House, though well-built, cannot accommodate all of his slaves. At the beginning of the Civil War, all of the planters left the island with the exception of Master Robert. Phineas Miller Nightingale, his closest neighbor, left not only the island behind but also two large houses on plantations he'd inherited—Oakland, and Dungeness, which originally belonged to General Nathaniel and Caty Greene. Dungeness, a four-story structure made of tabby with six-foot walls at the base, is an ideal place to house many of the slaves. During the 1813 storm, the building had survived intact. The roof blew off, but it was replaced with an expensive cooper roof. Master Robert knows it will offer protection. Oakland also withstood the famous storm of 1813. Both mansions are vacant.

"Tom, you take your people and get down to Dungeness. There are four floors. You will be crowded but safe, I hope."

Master Robert has confidence in his overseers. They know everyone they supervise and more important how to organize them into work gangs to accomplish the task at hand.

"Dido, you get your folks over to Oakland as quick as possible. The rain is just beginning to fall. No time to spare," he orders.

The slaves in Dido's group form into knots, like gaggles of geese.

"Let's go," Dido says.

They march southward—into the storm but toward the safety of Oakland. Mothers clutch their children by the hand. Babies carried in colorful slings of homespun fabric fuss as the first spits of rain spatter their faces. Heads down against the falling rain the strongest men lead the line of refugees.

"Phineas, the people who live in the slave quarters will have to share some space. They are brick and will stand up to the wind. Anyone that cannot be accommodated, send them to Planter's House," Mr. Robert says.

"Arabella, the hospital is a solid brick building," he says. "It made it through the last major storm. Move the male patients down from the second floor. They will be safer on the first."

Earlier in the week, the Bermuda High that controls summer weather for the southeastern United States dissipates. The clockwise rotation of the high prevents continental storms from sweeping over Cumberland Island. Until that time, storms are driven along a northerly route, subjecting the island to convective showers. Droughts often occur in July and August. But in the fall, the weather pattern changes in ways that are sometimes detrimental to the residents of the island. These changes are initiated to the south, in the Caribbean.

The Caribbean has a history of devastating hurricanes. In 1780, three major hurricanes strike within a two-week period. On October 3, the Jamaican town of Savanna-La Mar is leveled. On October 10 and 11, the Great Hurricane kills 4,326 people on Cumberland Island alone. That same storm tracks into French territory and sinks forty ships off Martinique, with a loss of five thousand sailors. And a third storm destroys a Spanish force of six dozen ships. It is ironic that the three world powers—Great Britain, France, Spain—competing for domination of the Americas are destroyed by hurricanes, not each other. Hurricanes account for more destruction of navies than the navies themselves.

Far to the south, a major cyclonic storm gathers energy over the hot waters of the Caribbean. Hispaniola receives eighteen inches of rain and driving winds. Out over open waters, the storm continues to intensify. Tracking to the northeast, it follows the North Equatorial Current and veers into the Florida Straits. To the east of Florida where the Gulf Stream begins, it explodes into an intense storm with destructive force winds. Bands of clouds race out ahead of the storm, two hundred to three hundred miles. Skirting the Florida coast, the storm heads for the coast of South Georgia. The waves that wash the beaches on Cumberland Island are generated from the winds wrapping the storm and traveling in excess of one hundred miles per hour.

The five horsemen of hurricanes—wind, hail, lightning, flood, and tornadoes—gallop toward Cumberland Island, as its residents seek emergency shelter. Trapped like minnows in a weir, each element is about to break loose and wreak havoc. Mr. Robert and the older slaves know what to expect. Though the wind will be loud and destructive, tearing large limbs from the largest and sturdiest of trees and frightening the children, the storm surge that will inundate large portions of the island is the most dangerous. Beaches, dunes, outbuildings, wharves, and the small boats the slaves use to ferry Union sailors up and down the sound soon will be washed out to sea.

"Amos, you and Amelia stay with me in Planter's House," Mr. Robert says. "We're on high ground, and the storm surge shouldn't affect us. I'm more concerned about the wind. The oaks will survive, but I am afraid that the loblolly pine and yellow pine will snap above the ground."

Amos stands on the veranda, looking out to the sound. He notices the change in the color of the sky. Earlier in the day, it was a hazy, coppery color. Now it is black with ominous, billowy clouds that rush toward him. Bright shafts of sunlight disappear, and the wind begins to stir. He hears the leaves rustle. At first softly, then gradually, the wind increases in intensity. It rattles the shutters on Planter's House, rapping the picture frames against the wall. The noise bothers him. The water in the sound changes from greenish blue to coal black. He notices the sharp contrast between the whitecaps pushed by the wind and the blackness of the sound. The wind blows from the southeast, pushing more and more water into the sound. Black and furious, the water rises rapidly and covers the docks, which Amos can no longer see.

"Untie those boats from the docks and get them to higher ground, or we will lose them in the swell," Master Robert yells to several field hands.

Three field hands, strong as oxen, race to the dock as rain pelts their muscular backs. Quickly, they untie the taut line, and drag the small boats away from the rising water.

"Amos, get away from that window," Master Robert yells. "If a limb blows in, you will be all cut up."

Tom and Dido reach their separate destinations—Dungeness and

Oakland—at about the same time, and just in time. The wind, as expected, blows out of the southeast. First, it tears small limbs from the sweet gum and hickory trees; then large branches snap and fall to the ground with great thuds. Leaves roil in the air, like flocks of black starlings splattered and stuck against the outside walls of the great estates. The walls shake. This frightens the small children, and they cry in terror as they clutch their mother's aprons.

"Calm, little babies. Calm, little babies," an old nurse sings. Soon the first floor of Dungeness is in song as mothers try to comfort their babies. The lullabies soothe the children despite the cacophony that bellows outside.

Tom knows the safest place in the house for the children is the first floor. The tabby walls at that level are six feet thick. Though the mansion has been unoccupied for several years, the furniture remains as it was when the owners departed.

"Look around. Look in the cupboards and sideboards. We need candles," Tom says. Most of the slaves are stunned. They have never been allowed in such a place and do not know where or what to look for.

"Here," a slave calls. "I have found a lamp. Perhaps it will light." The lamp is lit, and a soft glow radiates across the room. Someone else finds several candles in the drawer of a Sheraton sideboard. They are placed throughout the room and add comfort to the refugees, who huddle together. The field slaves look with wonder at the furniture and carpets.

All of a sudden, a bolt of lightning creates a flash so bright, it seems to be noontime. Seconds later, a loud peel of thunder rolls over the mansion. The vibration from the rumble frightens the children again. The ferocious wind howls and rattles the windows. Hinges snap as doors blow off storage sheds and outbuildings.

Somewhere out to sea, perhaps a hundred miles away, enormous forces are at work. More moisture from the warm currents feeds the storm from within, and it deepens. Instead of veering to the northeast, which is typical of storms in the South Atlantic Bight, it maintains its current course—due north toward Cumberland Island.

Mr. Robert paces the floor. The wind howls, and branch fall from the trees. "Amos, you come with me," he says. "We need to run over to the dairy and tell Long John to turn the animals loose. I don't want buildings crashing down on them. They will be safer on their own."

"Wow! Listen to the wind screech!" yells Amos as they open the door.

"This storm is only going to get worse," laments Mr. Robert. "But we still have time to save the livestock."

Long John, who supervises the livestock, stands by the door he has just closed. He hears Mr. Robert and Amos yelling. Mr. Robert and Amos run into the dairy barn. It is dry and smells of fresh straw and manure. The cows push against their pens. They are restless.

"John," Mr. Robert orders, "Open the doors, and let the cattle loose. I'm afraid the wind will collapse the roof and kill them."

John runs to the far end of the barn and pulls up an oak bar. He pushes the door open. Each of them run to individual pens and let the cows loose. The thunder startles the cattle. They push against each other, trying to escape. John stands behind the last one with an oak cane, swatting its backside to get it to move. A cacophony rises from the poultry pens.

"What about the poultry?" Amos asked.

"The chickens, ducks, and geese will be fine. I'll turn them loose so they can run to the woods," John says.

They run to the poultry pen. The noise is deafening. Chickens cluck. Roosters crow. Geese honk. Ducks quack. The geese flap their wings and waddle in the pen, while the chickens scurry helter-skelter from one corner to the other. Feathers fly erratically in the wind. For one minute, the rain falls in torrents, only to be followed by a break in the next. Panic spreads among the animals like the chains of lightning that flash between the peals of thunder. Cows, goats, hogs, and sheep herd together as they run for shelter in the maritime forest.

Amos thinks to himself, *I wonder if Noah felt like this before the great flood.*

"Amos, you get back to Planter's House. The animals will fend for themselves," Mr. Robert says.

Amos doesn't notice the intensity of the wind. He focuses on freeing the animals and poultry. Suddenly, a loud crash startles him. A thick branch snaps from a sweet gum tree and lands close by. The rain that follows the wind pelts his face. He is drenched. He dodges the large puddles that fill the main road as he races back to the safety of Planter's House.

Along the way, gusts of wind snap branches from trees. The wind howls and screams in his ears. It frightens him. He has never been in such foul weather. The rain and wind push him into the front door. Puddles follow as well. He stands dripping, but safe.

Master Robert and John barge through the front door right behind Amos. "John, check the hospital," Master Robert orders.

Between the maritime forest and the cotton fields, tall stands of loblolly and long-leaf pine sway in the wind. They rise sixty feet high and are two feet in diameter. The ground that supports them is spongy from the incessant rain. As John runs to the hospital, he hears a deafening roar and a series of loud thunderous crashes. In one fell swoop, the wind blows a swath of twenty pines to the ground. The black-green branches that reach for the sky look like the hand of a drowning man.

Out in the sound, the water continues to swell. A section of the dock and the roof of the boat house float past Planter's House. Debris fills the Intracoastal Waterway. Large trees and pieces of wreckage slam into the ships still anchored in the sound. The Union ships take a terrible beating. Although the sailors lower and tie all the sails, batten the hatches, and make fast the anchors, the force of the hurricane rips the sails and snaps the anchor lines. The rip tides push the ships and ground them on the sand bars. Like beached whales, they lie helpless. The Union Navy is vulnerable to attack. It will be days before the ships are righted, lines untangled, and masts repaired.

The small coastal port of Saint Mary's bears the brunt of the storm. The southeast wind churns the seas between the southern tip of Cumberland Island and Fort Clinch on the north Florida coast directly into the harbor. The storm surge rises thirteen feet. Anything that is not anchored is washed into Saint Mary's. Pilings, docks, wreckage, boats of all sizes, and outbuildings are smashed and broken. A long pile of strewn debris like tidal rack creates a ragged line across the town common. Many lives are lost. Many of the residents are swept away by the storm surge. By the time the hurricane moves away from South Georgia and skies clear, more than one thousand deaths are reported in Camden County.

The hurricane that sweeps the island is the first major calamity that affects Amos and Amelia, but not the last. As they grow toward adulthood, their lives will be tested many times due to events over which they have no control.

2

Zabette

The air is heavy; it is a heaviness that portends death. A shimmery haze gently sits on the flat water, obscuring the tall reeds and sea ducks that feed among them. Dots of large pink and white hibiscus flowers from marshmallow plants stand mute in the windless early morning. Marguerite Bernardy steps off the veranda of Plum Orchard, one of thirteen plantations on Georgia's Cumberland Island that prospered before the Civil War. She walks to the landing through an allée of live oak that frames a cotton field. The rising sun will be at its zenith this twenty-first day of June, 1847, the summer solstice, and blister the island in the afternoon, although, the morning mist has not yet evaporated. Apparitions dance like medieval performers at Carnival in the reeds. The island slaves see haints and ghosts in the interplay of light and moisture created by swamp and marsh miasma. Death follows these supernatural occurrences.

Aptly named the Low Country, Cumberland Island is the southernmost barrier island on the East Coast. It is an area of swamps, estuaries, sloughs, sand dunes, beaches, and lush maritime forests. The island has supported human habitation for thousands of years. Isolated from the mainland, it develops its own culture and practices, very different from those on the mainland. Men are creatures of the time in which they live, and take their color from the conditions that surround them, as the chameleon does from the grass or leaves in which it hides.

Marguerite enjoys this time of day. It is cool, and the few moments of solitary engagement afford her time to think. Today, her thoughts center on Planter's House, the adjoining plantation not far to the south. She knows the owner very well. Mr. Robert is a man of considerable intelligence and energy. For several decades she has observed him acquire property, grow cotton, and become prosperous. But now his life is troubled.

A brace of brown pelicans interrupts her thoughts as they skim low over the water. She follows the well-worn path back to the main house, enters the dining room, and fills a vase with wild flowers she has picked along the way. A mulatto slave, about nineteen years old, sets a silver platter on the cherry sideboard.

"Missy Bernardy, your tea … Oh, what beautiful flowers." She speaks softly.

"Zabette, pack some clothes. I'm sending you down to Planter's House. Mr. Robert's mother and sister are ill and will need your care," she says.

Marguerite Bernardy is a French slave owner who lives on the 1,240-acre Plum Orchard plantation. Her son, Pierre, bought it in 1823. Zabette, born in 1818, is the daughter of Pierre and his slave, Mary. Biologically, Zabette is Marguerite's granddaughter. Early in life, Zabette shows a keen intelligence and social skills. She is fluent in both French and English and is taught to read and write, illegal in the South at the time. By 1836, Zabette has trained as a nurse and acquires administrative skills in overseeing the duties of the main house. Her new position to care for Lucy Spaulding and her daughter, Susan Hawkins, an act of neighborly generosity, will change her life forever.

Marguerite orders her servant Peter to hitch up a carriage and transport Zabette to Planter's House, Mr. Robert's plantation.

The sun is high in the sky when Zabette climbs into the carriage. She feels the heat on her neck and shoulders.

"Giddy up!" yells Peter.

Zabette waves good-bye to Missy Bernardy, who stands on the porch and also waves good-bye. Suddenly Zabette feels apprehensive. She's never been away from Plum Orchard before.

"Are you all right?" asks Peter.

"I'm fine," Zabette assures him. "Just a bit nervous."

"Planter's House," says Peter. "Now there's a good place to work. Mr. Robert Stafford is a very successful planter. Everything he touches turns to gold."

Peter turns onto the road. It is tree-lined and creates shade and a gentle coolness. This is the only road on the island. It stretches the entire length of the eighteen miles from the north end to Beach Creek at the southern tip. This road has been used for two thousand years. Until the European incursion, Timacua Indians lived in relative peace on the island. Muddy during spring rains, the road is now dry and easy to travel.

Zabette notices everything along the way to Planter's House. Sweet gum, laurel oak, and tall southern yellow pine have replaced the live oak cut down thirty years earlier for the construction of frigates for the newly formed U.S. Navy. The sweet fragrance of climbing hemp wood, passion flower, and St. Andrew's cross fills her nostrils.

All of a sudden, an opening in the forest-lined road fills the buggy with sunshine. The shade from the forest canopy gives way to brilliant sunshine and a clear blue sky. Acres of open fields stand before them. Zabette sees cotton planted to the edge of the Atlantic Ocean on her left, and several smaller plots of rows of corn and beans on her right. Beyond the fields, a small herd of cattle graze in the shade of the trees in the forest.

"We're almost here!" Peter exclaims.

"Oh, my," Zabette says with a sigh. She is stunned by the magnificent house and grounds. The horse trots on the circular drive, which is shaded by carefully planted trees. Like an artist's palette, flowers bloom in a profusion of color. Reds, yellows, whites, and blues welcome the visitors. Date palms, with their long, lanced-shaped leaves, serve as a backdrop for the flowers. An orchard supports olive trees, oranges, and peaches. The house, substantial in size, commands two stories and is flanked on both sides by two massive chimneys. Across the field, directly in front of her, twelve red-brick slave cabins, each with its own chimney, nestle among the trees. Zabette thinks to herself, *This is indescribably beautiful, exotic, and semi-tropical.*

A tall cinnamon colored man stands by the door. He greets Peter and then says, "How do you do, missy?" He grabs Zabette's bag. "Master Robert is expecting you."

The massive door opens into a twelve-foot-wide hall. She enters Planter's House. Her feet feel the plush softness of a French Aubusson carpet stretched on a well-oiled heart-pine floor. Two Federal side chairs flank a rosewood sideboard. A Chinese porcelain vase filled with flowers draws her attention. She loves flowers.

A tall man in his mid-forties, blue-eyed with chestnut hair, walks into the entry. Very neatly dressed, he wears a pair of white linen trousers and a white cotton shirt. He takes off his gold-bowed spectacles and extends his hand in welcome.

"Zabette, I am pleased that Missy Bernardy sent you to care for my mother and sister," he says. He has just walked from the parlor. Zabette can see an extended rosewood table and large sideboard through the door.

"It's quite warm today ... Esther, please pour some tea," Mr. Robert says to one of the house servants.

"And how is Missy Marguerite?" he asks Zabette. "I haven't seen her since the Jonkonnu celebration.

""She is fine, sir. I am happy to be of service."

"After some refreshment, I will take you to my mother and sister."

Mr. Robert's mother, Miss Lucy, now seventy years old, has been ill for several months. Her health has steadily declined. Zabette slowly walks into the bedroom. The subtle smell of death wafts through the room and lingers gently in the air. In cold shadows, Miss Lucy lies still, enveloped in white linen. Her hair, white and brittle, has lost its youthful sheen. The pungent odor of medicines, astringents, and urine from the white porcelain chamber pot contrasts with the sweet smell of pomander balls in the other rooms. A beige shawl lies at the foot of her bed. A jaundiced face slowly turns and gazes into Zabette's eyes. Zabette takes note of the spidery blue veins that flow down Miss Lucy's forearms to the tops of her hands.

"It's so nice of you to come," she whispers.

"Let me get you something to drink," Zabette offers.

Miss Lucy slowly lifts the cup to her mouth; her gnarled fingers are barely able to grasp it. Slowly, she sips. "Enough," she says.

Mr. Robert ushers Zabette out of the room. She notices how neat and orderly he is. He moves like a lord. He is kind and gracious as he escorts her to his sister.

"Come with me. Mother is old and her time is short. She will die of old age … probably soon," he laments. "My sister, Susan, on the other hand, suffers from a high fever and is very ill."

Zabette follows Mr. Robert into Miss Susan's room. Sunlight fills the room. She immediately walks to Miss Susan's bedside and places the back of her hand on her forehead. It is hot. Miss Susan's eyes are glazed.

Zabette turns to Mr. Robert. "Tell me, when did she get sick?" she asks.

"About two weeks ago, she said she felt weak," he says. "She complained of a headache and did not want to eat. In fact, she ate very little. She said she had no appetite. And this week, the chills began."

Zabette holds Miss Susan's arm and notices it is trembling. She opens her nightdress and sees pink spots below her neck.

"How do you feel?" Zabette asks.

"I have cramps," Miss Susan replies feebly.

"She has typhoid fever, Mr. Robert, and she is very sick. I need to go into the woods and fetch some slippery elm and cramp bark. I will make slippery elm water and cramp bark tea. It will ease her pain … I'll be back soon," she says and leaves Planter's House.

The sun, brilliant with heat, is high in the sky. She walks down the circular drive, crosses a field and enters the understory of the maritime forest. Several plants and trees grow in abundance: sassafras, coralroot, and laurel cherry, known to the slaves for their medicinal uses. Zabette spots a tall slippery elm tree. It is indeed slippery. She reaches for her knife and carefully strips bark from the trunk. When she returns to the kitchen, she will pound the bark into a powder and add water. Zabette knows that slippery elm water will settle Miss Susan's stomach and cure her indigestion. She places the bark in a basket and searches for cramp bark. She soon finds the low-growing shrub with thick shiny leaves and dark berries used for holiday decorations. She pulls several plants from the moist forest floor. She will crush the roots in a mortar and make a tea to treat Miss Susan's cramps.

The shadow from Planter's House greets her as she returns from her herbal foraging in the forest. The sun is low in the sky, but the air is warm as an oven. Earlier in the day, Zabette is awed by the property. Now, she is intent on preparing the herbs for Miss Susan's treatment. Mr. Robert, waits on the veranda, seated in his favorite rocking chair and reading a newspaper, as she steps up to the door.

"Zabette, did you get the herbs you need?" he asks.

"Yes, sir!" she replies.

"Zabette, tomorrow I will sail to Savannah. I have business up there. You will remain at Planter's House and take care of my mother and sister. Esther—she's the one who served us tea—will get you whatever you need."

A successful planter and businessman, Robert Stafford overcame the stinging prejudice of social class in plantation society through hard work and intelligence. He possessed an intuitive sense of the geography of the island, perhaps because he grew up on it.

His father, Thomas, and Uncle Robert worked for General Nathaniel Greene and his wife, Caty. General Greene was George Washington's Southern general during the American Revolution, and they were good friends. In 1800, when Robert was ten years old, his father died. Because Thomas Stafford believed that males and females in his family should inherit equal shares of his property, he named his wife Lucy sole executrix of his estate. Lucy soon remarried Isham Spaulding and in August 1800 purchased 125 acres from the Nathaniel Greene estate.

The two families know each other well. Robert Stafford is a friend of Nathaniel (Nat) Ray Greene and Nat's sisters, Louisa and Cornelia, children of General Nathaniel Greene. And those relationships ensure his success as a planter. Cornelia Littlefield Greene sells six hundred acres of tract 5 on Cumberland Island to the Staffords in 1813. Tract 5 is a valuable purchase and shows Robert's business sense. It consists of the two kinds of swamps favored by rice planters: an inland swamp and a freshwater tidal swamp. The area had been reclaimed years before by rice planters. The labor of cutting trees and draining land had already been completed. Stafford uses his purchase to cultivate Sea Island cotton. When he makes this initial purchase, his family has five slaves. By the beginning of the Civil War in 1860, his estate has grown to 110 slaves and covers a large portion of Cumberland Island.

Robert Stafford's prosperity rises like a peregrine falcon on a thermal as cotton becomes a major world commodity. Cumberland Island is uniquely suited to the growth of cotton. The combination of climate, soil, and the rich detritus from the salt marshes makes it possible to exact huge profits from Sea Island cotton. Between 1784 and 1850, cotton imported to England rises from twenty million pounds (none from North America) to 1.5 billion pounds (82 percent from Dixie), a 150-fold increase in demand. Cotton exports in 1850 amount to $80 million. In 1860, sales of cotton earn more than two and one half times as much—more than the entire US export trade in all commodities and manufacturing. Cotton is truly king, and Robert is master of his domain.

This newfound prosperity has severe consequences, however—not only for Robert but for plantation society as well. By 1836, the tariffs of 1824 and 1828 imposed by the North are affecting the profitability of Southern cotton. To prevent the erosion of his profits, Robert purchases a textile mill in the North. He manufactures "negro cloth," a rough fabric used to make clothes for slaves, and sells it at a profit.

Mr. Robert's trip to Savannah involves not the planting of cotton but the movement of cotton to Savannah, from where it is shipped all over the world. He meets several prominent businessmen interested in investing in the construction of a railroad from inland Georgia to the port of Savannah. In 1830, Peter Cooper produces the first

American-built steam locomotive. Three years later, the state issues a charter that drops construction of canals in favor of rails. In 1835, construction begins on the Central Rail Road of Georgia. Mr. Robert grasps the concept immediately and realizes that it will be possible to transport bales of cotton from inland Georgia to the coast. He strikes at this opportunity and becomes an early investor of railroads in Georgia. But first, land has to be cleared and rail beds built, an expensive endeavor. Rather than invest his own capital, he provides his slaves as labor instead. This costs him very little and in return, he receives shares in the new railroad. He is a successful business man at the age of forty-three and has unlimited opportunities to acquire more wealth. But he lacks one thing—a family.

The following morning Mr. Robert sets sail for Savannah from the dock at Planter's House. A slight breeze blows from the west, promising a fine day.

"I'll be gone several days," he tells Esther and Zabette. "Take care of Mother and Missy Susan until I return."

Zabette and Esther stand together on the wharf and wave good-bye. They are both tall and thin—one has an ebony complexion, the other is a creamy mocha, reflecting the interracial coupling in a frontier society. The sun is still low in the sky as they walk back to Planter's House. Hues of pink dance on the ripples left in the wake of Mr. Robert's small sloop, *Amelia*. Zabette looks back as the sloop sails away and thinks of the freedom it affords. She is nineteen and has never been off the island. Her entire life centers on the chores and responsibilities at Plum Orchard. She watches the *Amelia* sail up the sound with sails as white as bleached oyster shells. For the first time in her life, she wonders if she could leave the island. But how?

"Esther, how often does Master Robert sail to Savannah?" she asks.

"Oh, Master Robert travels a lot. He has business in Savannah and also in Connecticut," Esther replies.

"Connecticut? Where is that?"

"Way up north. I have never been there. He owns a textile mill. He goes for a month or two when he goes to Connecticut," Esther says.

While Mr. Robert meets with railroad investors in Savannah,

Zabette cares for Miss Lucy and Miss Susan. Day by day, she watches Miss Lucy slowly lose her strength and her voice get softer and more gravely. She needs help drinking from a cup and eats very little. Miss Susan's condition is more volatile—chills one day and fever the next. Slippery elm water and cramp bark tea ease the pain but do not cure the typhoid fever.

A few days later the *Amelia* is sighted by field hands. They join in song to welcome Mr. Robert back to Planter's House. He jumps from the sloop onto the dock and immediately visits his mother and Miss Susan. Miss Susan lies still, her eyes closed. She does not respond to his greeting. He walks to her side and feels her pulse. Her wrist is clammy. Otherwise, there is nothing.

"Zabette, Miss Susan has passed," he laments. "The fever was more than she could stand."

Zabette and Esther prepare the body and lay her out on the parlor table. The funeral is held a day later. Late afternoon thunderstorms summon torrential rains and high winds, followed by loud crashes of thunder and brilliant lighting strikes. The humidity suffocates the mourners. Beads of sweat roll from their foreheads and saturate their clothing. The temperature rises, and the air remains hot, moist, and unstable. Three weeks later Miss Lucy passes. In a short time, Mr. Robert loses both his mother and his sister.

Mr. Robert mourns quietly in the parlor. He sits, shoulders hunched and head down. The room is dark. Zabette, aware of his loss, walks up behind him and put her hands on his shoulders. In his lap lies his mother's Bible. It is open to Psalm 23. The pages are worn and brown with age. A profound sadness wraps around him like a boa constrictor. His eyes are red and swollen. Tears flood down his cheek and onto the Bible.

> The Lord is my shepherd; I shall not be in want. He makes me to lie down in green pastures, he leads me beside quiet waters, he restores my soul. He guides me in the path of righteousness for his name's sake. Even though I walk through the valley of the shadow of death, I will fear no evil,

for you are with me; your rod and your staff, they comfort
me. You prepare a table before me in the presence of my
enemies. You anoint my head with oil; my cup overflows.
Surely goodness and love will follow me all the days of my
life, and I will dwell in the house of the Lord forever. (Psalm
23:1–6)

He is immobilized, unable to speak. Yet her touch awakens a strong
feeling in him. For the next several days, a hush falls over Planter's
House. Mr. Robert loses his enthusiasm. He eats little. He avoids people
and does not conduct business. He truly is in the doldrums, the wind
taken out of his sail.

Zabette tries to cheer him up. She fills the many cut glass vases
with flowers; zinnias, asters, and nasturtiums brim bright with color.
She throws the drapes open to let sunlight stream into the rooms. The
cut glass vases sparkle. Slowly, the brightness and optimism she creates
affects his behavior. Each day he shows signs that his grief is receding.
His appetite increases, and he laughs again.

"Zabette," Mr. Robert announces one sunny morning. "I want
you to stay here at Planter's House and work for me. I'll talk to Miss
Bernardy. I am sure we can work out an arrangement. I am grateful to
you for the care you gave my mother and sister. They managed Planter's
House, and I need someone who is equal to that task."

And with that announcement Zabette's new home is Planter's House.
Mr. Robert's gratitude for Zabette's services soon turns to affection. She
fills the void he felt at his mother's and sister's death. He is struck by her
physical beauty. She moves effortlessly through the house like a zephyr.
Unlike the field slaves whose hands are rough and language crude,
Zabette's are smooth as a lettered olive shell, and she speaks with a lilt.
And when she speaks, her eyes flash. The fact that Zabette is a mulatto
does not concern Mr. Robert. In fact, Mr. Robert is not concerned with
the opinions of others. However, the state of Georgia is quite clear about
interracial relationships. They are forbidden.

The oppressive heat of summer slowly dissipates, and cool breezes
from the North sweep across the island. Zabette marvels at the pink

trumpet-shaped false foxgloves and loves the St. Andrew's cross. She picks the blue Maypop flowers that bloom in the fall along the wood's edge as she travels through the maritime forest to the beach and back. She enjoys the cool weather and looks forward to the holidays. This year, in particular, she looks forward to hosting both Christmas and Jonkonnu with Mr. Robert.

Zabette becomes the mistress of Planter's House. She is efficient and deals with the slaves fairly, although she does not allow field slaves in the main house. They wait outside. Between Mr. Robert's entrepreneurial spirit and Zabette's management skills, Planter's House and its inhabitants expand and flourish.

Mr. Robert entertains a variety of influential people—his family, business associates, and politicians. "When the weather cools in the fall," he tells Zabette one sunny afternoon. "I want to invite many of my friends from the Camden Hunting Club and two bankers from Saint Mary's to Planter's House, perhaps the weekend of the boat races. I fully expect my crew to win again this year. It will be a pleasure to celebrate their win."

Mr. Robert has many interests and hobbies. He loves to hunt and fish in the marshes and estuaries on Cumberland Island and on his friends' plantations on the mainland. Many of the wealthy planters love to gamble. One of their pursuits is a friendly competition between the members of the Camden Hunting Club. They each sponsor a crew of their slaves and have boat races in the fall and spring. Often Mr. Robert's crew wins the event.

When the day arrives, Zabette instructs the servants to prepare a sumptuous meal of oysters, venison, and wild duck. She personally fills the vases with wild flowers. Candles are lit, and a honey glow is cast over the room. At the end of the meal, Mr. Robert speaks. "Zabette, you take the women in to the parlor, and I will join the men in the library for Madeira and cigars."

"Gentlemen, I am delighted you came to visit this evening, and I hope you enjoyed the meal," he says. "But I do want to talk about business."

He turns first to a business associate, Darcy, a banker from Saint Mary's. "Darcy, why do you foreclose on your neighbors?"

Although surprised by the bluntness of the question, Darcy responds immediately. "Robert, that's quite clear. My *neighbors*," he says sarcastically, "don't meet their obligations. We, that is the bank, extend a loan … say for $2,500 to be paid in three installments over a three-year period. To protect ourselves, we require the borrower to present some insurance, usually a piece of property or the equivalent value in slaves. If they cannot meet their obligation within three years, we have no alternative but to foreclose. After all the bank shareholders need to be protected. Robert, we auction the property and the slaves."

"Yes, that's true … but at a loss, "Mr. Robert responds. "The bank loses money, and the land owner loses property and slaves. Everybody loses. I have been a planter on the island for many years … both good years and lean years. Some things you can't control … weather, for instance. Remember three seasons ago when we had that late torrential rain. It ruined that year's crop. In fact, I lost 30 percent of my Sea Island cotton that year. If I could not make payments to you, you would own my plantation. And what would you do with it?" Mr. Robert asks.

"Well, of course, we would put it on the auction block," Darcy's face reddens as he puffs his cigar. "Robert, business is business."

"I see," says Mr. Robert. "So, you end up with a property and perhaps some slaves. You are not a farmer … what do you know about the farming business? What happens to the land? And what happens to the slaves?"

Mr. Robert is aware of the problems inherent in an agricultural economy that is heavily dependent upon borrowed money. As he talks with his business associates, he glances into the dining room and notices the table. Zabette has extended it to accommodate the guests. He slowly rises from his chair, offers his guests another glass of Madeira, and walks into the dining room. He slides his hand along the table as he walks its length.

Extension. What if I could extend those loans for three to five more years? I could make money on the interest, and the mortgage holder could continue his business until he was in a position to repay the loan, he thinks to himself. And that's exactly what he did.

Between 1840 and 1850, Mr. Robert increases his fortune by

loaning money to planters on the island and investors on the mainland. As a planter, he understands the uncertainty of weather, which often results in severe crop looses. While a bank forecloses on a property if payment cannot be met a harvest time, Mr. Robert extends the note for several years, in some cases as many as nine years with 6 percent interest on the debt. He makes loans of $2,000 to $8,000. Slaves or land are put up as security, and if a creditor defaults. Mr. Robert receives the property or slaves through foreclosure. Even with his generous extensions, at some point in time, debts have to be paid. He loans his neighbors amounts that range from $350 to $1,500 and investors on the mainland—who invest in banks, railroads, and canals in northern Florida and southeastern Georgia—between $2,000 and $10,000.

Like mares' tails that form on the horizon after a cold front, setting the conditions for violent storms, two issues force Mr. Robert to make a difficult decision. The first is his age. He is fifty-five years old, has amassed a fortune, and can very easily lose it. The second is that the Congress of the United States has passed the controversial Fugitive Slave Act. Robert and Zabette raised six children together on the island. The entire family will be affected by this law. As long as Zabette remains on the island, she has no legal protection. The state of Georgia does not recognize their relationship. Because she is a mulatto, her children will not receive any protection either if something happens to Mr. Robert.

"Robert, why are you moping about?" Zabette asks one sultry afternoon.

"Zabette, come here," he replies. "I am very concerned about you and the children. If something should happen to me, you will immediately become poor. The state will take all this property and auction it to the highest bidder. You and the children will be left nothing."

The twinkle in Zabette's eyes dims, and her expression turns from smiling to concerned. "What are you telling me?" she asks.

"I am sending you and the children north to live in Connecticut," he says. "I have thought about this for a long time and have made proper arrangements. I have acquired a house for you and school for the children."

In response to the fugitive slave laws passed in the South, Connecticut passes a personal liberty law. To protect his family, Mr. Robert will move them eight hundred miles away. In the same way slave masters broke up families, the laws in the antebellum south will separate Mr. Robert from his family.

"But what about us?" Tears fill Zabette's eyes.

"I will visit several times a year," he assures her.

Zabette thinks about this for a long time. Years before she'd wanted her freedom. For the first time since the day she saw Mr. Robert sail to Savannah, hope stirs in her heart. Now, she will have her freedom; but at what cost? Connecticut is so far from the island. *This is the land I know so well. It is cold in Connecticut, and I know no one*, she thinks.

3

Evacuation

After Mr. Robert moves his family to Connecticut, he is constantly troubled. He feels an ache. He sorely misses Zabette and the children. Once a year, he sails to Connecticut to meet with the manager of his textile mill and conduct business at two of his banks. He always looks forward to the visit with his family. Each year he is amazed as he watches his six children grow taller.

"You all will be as tall as a loblolly pine," he tells them. "What about school? Let's see how well you are doing."

He questions them on sentence structure, grammar, and computational skills. He loves Zabette and the children and is sad when the time comes for him to return to Planter's House on the island.

Zephia, a house servant at Planter's House, gives birth to twins—Amos and Amelia. As young children they are raised in the plantation nursery. Every day, when Zephia completes her chores, she goes to spend time with them. Mr. Robert takes a special interest in these children.

"Zephia, how are Amos and Amelia?" he always asks.

Mr. Robert enjoys watching them grow. He notices they both take a keen interest in everything around them. When they are toddlers, Amos babbles and points every time a bird flies over, and Amelia is attracted to insects crawling on leaves. When they grow older, they ask myriad questions to any adult who has the misfortune of encountering them.

"Why do some trees have gnarly branches and others are tall and straight?" Amos asks. Amelia is interested in colors. "Why are all the flowers different?"

When the children are old enough, Mr. Robert takes them in his buggy whenever he supervises the planting of cotton or rides to the north end of the island to check on the timber operations. Soon the slaves say that Master Robert has found his children.

Thud! The bow of the *Amelia*, Mr. Robert's small sailboat slaps against the waves. Like a fine sleet, a brisk breeze from the North pelts Amos's and Amelia's faces as they huddle together in the bow. The chilly wind cuts through their homespun shirts to the marrow of their bones. They are sailing to the port of Fernandina. White caps splash against the hull. The spray cascades high in to the air.

"Amos, you and Amelia keep your eyes alert, and let me know if you see a sand bar," booms Mr. Robert's voice from the stern. His voice challenges the roar of the wind. Sandbars in the sound are treacherous and have grounded many a ship that tries to navigate it. Like the tide, the sandbars change daily. Expert ferrymen are required to navigate ships up and down the sound from the Satilla River to Saint Mary's and Fernandina.

"Mr. Robert, I don't see any sandbars." Amelia turns to him, her hair whipped by the wind. "But there's Fernandina just ahead!"

Fernandina, a small coastal port, sits at ocean level, floating like a humpback whale amid desolate windswept marshes. Located at the mouth of Saint Andrews Sound, where Georgia and Florida meet, Fernandina is protected by Fort Clinch.

A year earlier in 1859, the Fernandina Volunteers, a local militia, seize the fort. It is unoccupied at the time, but they install fortified artillery batteries on the beaches and armaments sent from Fort Marion in Saint Augustine. Shortly afterward, Robert E. Lee visits the coastal defenses of the South from the Carolinas to Saint Augustine. Shocked by the conditions at Fort Clinch, he writes a pessimistic letter to his daughters, recounting his observations:

> I have been down the coast as far as Amelia Island to examine
> our defenses. They are poor indeed and I have laid off work

enough to employ our people for a month. I hope our enemy will be polite enough to wait for us. It is difficult to get our people there to realize their positions. The volunteers dislike work and there is much sickness. The rifled cannon had now come into use and masonry forts such as Fort Clinch were indefensible. That coupled with Florida's remoteness from the primary theaters of war and lack of strategic significance, I will recommend that all troops be withdrawn from the coastal areas.

Although his plantation is almost self-sufficient, Mr. Robert still needs to purchase several items. In his pocket he carries a list that reads molasses, salt, sugar, salted fish, brandy, rum, and tobacco. Amos and Amelia often accompany him when he takes his sailboat to buy supplies for the plantation. Though they are young, they are strong, intelligent, and reliable. Little did they know how their lives would intersect with Fort Clinch and the Union Navy. Off to the east, like a hurricane in the Atlantic Ocean, the largest naval amphibious landing in US history is forming to blockade the port of Fernandina and Cumberland Island.

Clouds scud across the slate-gray sky. Dark ripples from the wake in the gray-green water look like slithering snakes—an ominous sign. The sail flaps loudly as the relentless wind pushes the boat on its course. As they sail closer to Fernandina, Amelia Island becomes distinct from the mainland. The long trestle bridge that connects the port to inland Florida stretches like a ribbon. Buildings loom ahead and cast shadows in the water. A long, wooden-plank dock stretches into the inlet to greet them. The pungent smells of turpentine and tar permeate the air. Mr. Robert maneuvers the boat alongside of one of the many wharfs.

"Amelia, you toss the stern line, and I'll get the bow," yells Amos. The twins skillfully toss both lines over two pilings, jump onto the dock, and make the lines taut.

"Good job!" says Mr. Robert. "Let's get out of this wind."

Standing on the dock, Amos looks around. "Where is everybody?" The dock area, usually a beehive of activity, is conspicuously quiet. Usually old black men with nimble fingers sit in the shade of the warehouses, deftly mending fishing nets. But they are absent. No one runs to greet them and exchange news. Barrels of fish bait stand on the dock, unattended. Only the sea gulls that screech and circle the dock, scavenging for food and fighting with each other, welcome them to Fernandina.

"Let's get up to the warehouse and find out," replies Mr. Robert. "We can also warm up."

Amelia yells to Amos, "Beat you to the warehouse!" They both sprint to the end of the dock. Mr. Robert follows more slowly. Amelia jumps onto the dirt road one step ahead of Amos and runs directly to one of several large warehouses that wrap the harbor. They both touch the door at the same time.

Mr. Robert yells, "You two wait for me!"

A large green sign with bold gold lettering beckons them: Ackerman's Supplies. The twins push the large door open and fall into the warm room. They are relieved to be out of the wind.

"Hello, anybody here?" they call. Not a sound. Amos's sharp black eyes scan the large room. Smells of tobacco, sassafras, and peppermint arouse his nostrils. There are crates stamped Nassau and Havana in large black letters, wooden barrels stuffed with pork, boxes of all sizes, bolts of cotton and linen fabric, canvas, and hemp line, but no clerk.

Mr. Robert enters the room and steps on a newspaper lying on the floor. He stoops to pick it up. "Federal Gunboats Steam for Fernandina," blurts out the headline.

"Amos and Amelia, listen to this. The newspaper says we're at war." He reads to them. "President Abraham Lincoln orders naval blockade of all southern ports. That includes us. It also says that General Braxton Bragg has ordered the Confederate States Army to evacuate East Florida and report to Tennessee. This means they will be no army to protect us. It looks like we are on our own."

In April 1861, the year before, Fort Sumter in Charleston, South Carolina, is attacked, and the Civil War begins. Five days later, Lincoln orders the naval blockade. Today, no one knows when the final curtain of the war will fall. Nor does anyone envision William T. Sherman's march to the sea and its devastating consequences to plantation society.

Amos and Amelia rush to the door. They hear loud shouts and see people running helter-skelter in every direction. Some carry bags; others small pieces of furniture. Dogs bark and small children cry. Amos sees a white boy about his age struggling with a large upholstered chair.

"Where is everybody going?" he shouts.

"The Yankees are coming! The Yankees are coming! Get out while you can!"

Unknown to Mr. Robert, Confederate forces have been ordered to evacuate Amelia Island. Earlier in the week, the Confederate garrison at Fort Clinch received orders to dismantle the guns and haul them inland. They remove the artillery pieces from Fort Clinch and transport them across the bridge to the mainland. The retreating soldiers spike fourteen of the guns and burn their carriages. Eighteen guns are sent to defend Savannah.

Unaware that the Union armada is steaming toward them, the residents do not take the evacuation warnings seriously. Colonel Hopkins of the 4th Florida Infantry is furious. When the locals do not pay attention to his notice to evacuate, he issues a second notice on March 1: "A special notice, to wit, that on Sunday March 2, at 10:00 a.m., a special train will leave the city expressly for the transportation of all women and children desirous of leaving." But among a few residents, the warning falls on deaf ears.

A train whistle screams; first, one long blast, then two short blasts. Mr. Robert looks toward the train depot, where a large unruly crowd gathers. The train belches and billows puffs of white smoke and steam. People push and shove to get onto the train. Finally, with a final blast of the whistle, it slowly pulls away from the depot.

Another large crowd congregates in the town square. Rumors fly like brown bats leaving a cave. *Where are the Yankees? Has anyone seen them?* The sound of hoof beats in the distance gets louder and louder. Several men gallop into the square shouting, "We can see their boats! We can see their boats!" Their horses are lathered because they've been ridden hard, their reigns as tight as coiled wire from the strain. A black informant has relayed a message to federal forces that the fort is being evacuated and that many of the town's people are leaving as well.

Piles of household items stand quietly in sharp contrast to the frenzied activity of the people. White planters shout orders to their black servants. Like wild-eyed horses in a barn fire, the crowd panics. Church bells ring in alarm. A crowd of women, children, old men, black, white, slave, and free follows the soldiers across the bridge to the safety of the mainland. Mr. Robert senses danger and tells Amos and Amelia to get back to the boat and prepare to sail home.

"When this is over, we'll come back and get what we need. Now is not the time," he tells Amos and Amelia.

The twins release the lines. They straddle the gunnels with one foot and push the boat away from the dock. When they are safe in the boat, they assume their positions. Still blowing from the north, the wind has not abated. Amelia raises the sail. Amos yells, "Ready about!" Sailing into the wind is a difficult task and requires a skillful skipper.

The war has had little effect on the civilians in South Georgia and Florida over the past year, but that is about to change. In November 1861, Sherman captures Port Royal, South Carolina, from Confederate forces. In a letter to General McClellan on December 19, 1861, he writes, "Admiral Du Pont thinks he will be ready for Fernandina in a week or two. I have a long time been ready for Fernandina, but the Navy is not."

Finally, on February 28, 1862, the Union fleet sets sail for Fernandina. Located at the end of the Florida Railroad terminus, Fernandina is a military target. Georgia's coastal islands are not prepared, and the residents are defenseless. For the first time, plantation owners in this part of the South will feel the effects of the blockade and the consequences of secession. Like Pandora's box, the war is unleashed with all its chaos and confusion. Amos and Amelia also will be victims, caught up in events beyond their control, their lives changed forever.

Mr. Robert raises a pair of binoculars to his eyes and scans the horizon. He sees a long line of ships steaming toward them. At first, they appear low on the horizon, but soon he can clearly see their smokestacks and flags. Smoke that billows from their stacks quickly dissipates due to the wind.

"Amos ... Amelia! I can see white flashes from their guns. Listen to the sound. They are firing on the town!" he yells.

When the skeleton crew at Fort Clinch sees the armada, they fire two or three cannon rounds and quickly depart. From the shore, a few remaining Confederate soldiers fire random musket shots at the gunboats, but there is no organized resistance.

A small river steamer, smoke pouring from its funnels, attempts to escape to Saint Mary's. An old woman in a calico sunbonnet waves a white flag from one of the piers. The train that has just left the station slowly gathers speed and begins to cross the long trestle bridge that connects the island with the mainland. Passengers hoot, jeer, and wave handkerchiefs derisively from the train-car windows. A federal gunboat fires several shots at the train, aiming at the locomotive. A cacophony of shots booms through the air. Missiles in long, swooping arcs explode over the train. One finds its mark. A cannon ball explodes in the last car. It splinters tables, chairs, and bedsteads and kills two boys seated on a sofa. Two men are also killed when a shell explodes on their flatcar. The crew jump from the locomotive and detach the car. Leaving its victims to face cannon shots, it steams to safety.

Another federal gunboat pursues the small river steamer. Mr. Roberts realizes that the federals might also chase him down as well.

"Amos, turn about!" he orders. "Sail us back to the dock."

When the twins reef the sail, he says, "Better stay put. No sense risking our lives."

From their small sailboat, Mr. Robert and the twins watch in horror as the federal gunboat chases down the river steamer. Amos and Amelia have never witnessed anything like this. Both boats sail at full steam. Smoke billows out of their stacks. The federal steamer has a large side-paddle wheel that furiously pushes the water and propels her closer and closer to the small boat.

"Amelia!" Amos yells. "This looks like a boat race."

"Yeah! A dangerous one," she responds.

They watch the federal skipper overtake the steamer and maneuver alongside. Several sailors board the steamer. On board, forty women and children are on their knees in prayer. "Deliver us from the Yankees," they pray. Ironically, the skipper of the river steamer is a Yankee from New England.

"Amos and Amelia," Mr. Robert calls. "Let's get back in town and find a room for the night. We'll need permission to leave safely, and that won't be for a while."

Federal troops land the next morning. Soon the town is filled with Yankees; members of the 4th New Hampshire, 9th Maine, and 97th Pennsylvania capture the city. Chaos and confusion reign in Fernandina. Amos and Amelia watch as soldiers plunder in all directions. Sailors and marines from the fleet assist and seem to have reduced the system of pillage to an exact science. Sailors drunk with success succumb to disorderly conduct. The few inhabitants who remain on the island are boarded up in their homes, terrified.

When reports reach Captain Towle, the Union commander, that the drinking has gotten out of hand, he orders all liquor on the island to be confiscated. Shortly afterward, a ship docks at the port with a cargo of whiskey.

"I want all the whiskey on that ship rolled onto the dock and the barrels smashed," Towle orders. Sailors break open the barrels with axes and pour the contents into the harbor, to the delight of the fish.

Twenty-five or thirty of the families who remain in town are loyal to the Yankees. They are treated well. Several make money by selling their wares to the invaders. The federal troops post a notice that reads "Persons and property of the Loyal will not be molested." They seize a large supply of rice, cotton, whiskey, molasses, and turpentine. They also confiscate a locomotive, several railroad cars, and two blockade runners filled with cargo.

Despite the excitement of the invasion, Mr. Robert eats breakfast at the boarding house with Amos and Amelia. The smell of fried pork, bacon, corn grits, eggs, and biscuits wafts through the small dining room. As the twins pour cane syrup on their biscuits, Mr. Roberts asks for another cup of hot steaming coffee. The owner graciously pours Mr. Robert another cup and tells a black servant to clear the dishes.

"What do you suppose will happen to us?" she asks Mr. Robert.

"I am about to find out," he replies. "I'll speak with the commander of these forces and find out what their intentions are." He turns to the twins. "You two wait here for me. I'll be back soon."

He briskly steps down the main street to find the commander's headquarters, but then he hears a loud commotion. A group of bellicose women taunt several federal troops and attempt to take down the American flag. The commander in charge of the flag detail is frustrated by their behavior. "You seem to have mistaken courage for treason and have a theatrical desire to figure as heroines," he shouts at them

"The men here are cowards," the women yell. "But we are not!" They make one last attempt to take down the flag. The officer gives the final order. "Men, get these women off the streets."

With the exception of the patriotic women, no one in the town is detained by the troops. Those who remain are Union sympathizers. Union men give the Union oath of allegiance and are permitted to return to their homes. Amos and Amelia watch the activity from the porch of the boarding house. They see several black men appeal to Union officers to be allowed to join their ranks. They are turned away.

In the meantime, Mr. Robert finds Captain Towle and requests permission to sail back to Cumberland Island, unharmed.

"Sir, tell me what you do on the island?" Captain Towle asks.

"I am a planter. I grow crops, primarily cotton and raise livestock," Mr. Robert tells him.

The commander expresses a great deal of interest in his plantation. "You know, we are going to need food to supply this flotilla, lots of men to feed. Perhaps you would agree to enter into a contract with the federal government. Do you think you have enough livestock and vegetables to supply our needs?"

"I do!" Mr. Robert replies.

Later, as the war unfolds, Mr. Robert follows its progress. He receives newspapers from Savannah on a regularly basis and reads all of the articles diligently. Unlike Confederate sympathizers, he believes the war will last a long time. He has a cotton mill in the North and interests in several banks in Connecticut, which provide him a perspective many Southerners do not have. He has confidence in the industrial might of the North. As a businessman, he has fought against secession from the beginning, because he realizes the devastating consequences it will have for trade. Here is an opportunity, he thinks, to survive the war and perhaps even make some money.

"Sir, I appreciate this opportunity to conduct business with you," Captain Towle says.

"In a few days, let's meet at my plantation and discuss the specifics of your proposal," Mr. Robert suggests.

Captain Towle turns to Mr. Robert and says, "Sir, tomorrow on the first tide, I will provide an escort to get you safely across Saint Andrew's Sound.

Near nightfall, several hundred Confederate irregular troops join forces with refugees on the mainland; under orders from General Trapier, they burn any property that might be of use to the enemy. Much of the property is owned by Union sympathizers who had recently immigrated to the area and set up businesses. At dusk, torches are applied to sawmills and warehouses. Vandalism accompanies this destruction. Many Union sympathizers flee back to Fernandina for safety.

A new threat emerges as a result of the war. A group of men gather like swill in a bucket, calling themselves "regulators." They are neither Confederate nor Union soldiers; they are malcontents who thrive in the maelstrom of chaos. When the Confederate forces move to Tennessee, these lawless men loot and burn property. From the porch of their boarding house, Amos and Amelia watch an eerie glow shoot into the sky—flames from the property that burns on the mainland. The following morning, Union soldiers report seeing many charred ruins of smoldering buildings—torched the night before. The war that has been lying in wait finally comes to Cumberland Island and Mr. Robert's plantation.

4

Warning

The night sky turns from its blue-black, ink-blot color to a misty gray as dawn slowly creeps to begin a new day. The starry skies, particularly the constellation Orion, fade into the morning dawn. Amos is in the kitchen boiling coffee for Mr. Robert. He is deeply troubled. Like seaweed caught on rocks, his mind is tangled. He remembers the invasion of Fernandina a few months earlier and the violence and chaos it produced. He can still hear the crying children and the smell of burning buildings. *Will Amelia and I be caught up in events like that,* he wonders. His thoughts are interrupted.

"Amos!" booms Robert Stafford's voice.

"Yes, Master Robert."

"Let's go on down to Raccoon Keys and check on that marsh gang. It's almost light, and the tide should be about right. Get the buggy!"

Amos rushes to the stable, pulls two marsh tackies from their stall, and hitches them to the wagon. In his left hand, he holds the reigns, and with his right, he grabs the whip. He snaps the whip lightly and pulls the team to Mr. Robert, who closes the front door. Mr. Robert stands tall as he waits on the veranda. He wears a pair of white cotton trousers, white shirt, and a full-brimmed straw hat.

"It's going to be another hot one, I can feel it," quips Mr. Robert as he pulls a bandanna from his back pocket and wipes his forehead. "Let's get this done before the sun climbs too high."

Amos drives the team down the dusty work road toward the marsh. They pass through the maritime forest filled with stands of live oak. The tree branches curve upward and outward, holding large sheets of Spanish moss, like laundry. In the early light, the muted silver-gray moss gives Amos an eerie feeling. He hears a crack in the forest. His neck hairs stand on edge. What is it? Possibly a deer … there are many on the island. Perhaps an ole raccoon coming home from his nightly rounds, or maybe something else … or someone.

Just a few days earlier, Mr. Robert reminds Amos to be vigilant. "We're in for some troubled times, Amos," Mr. Robert tells him. "Ever sense the Union Navy sailed into the sound and invaded Fernandina, there's been trouble on the mainland. Unsavory people are raising mischief. If you see anything unusual, be sure to tell me."

"Yes, sir, Mr. Robert."

Abraham Lincoln's blockade of the Southern states that seceded from the Union—South Carolina, Georgia, Alabama, Florida, Mississippi, and Texas—begins. Twenty-four steam ships and eight vessels sail into the sound accompanied by one infantry brigade, comprised of the 97th Pennsylvania and the 4th New Hampshire.

The Union commanders—unaware of the many obstacles to navigating the seemingly placid waters of Cumberland Sound—run aground. The ribbon of blue stretching between two verdant shorelines appears to be an easy drill for naval operations. Unseen beneath the waters, however, two opposing forces meet. With each tidal change, the sand bars shift unpredictably. Only three of the Union vessels navigate the sound and make it to Fernandina. Many of the others find themselves stuck on the sand bars like beached whales.

This problem becomes another economic opportunity for Mr. Robert. Not only is he able to sell produce and meat to the Union forces, he will soon lease his slaves to the Union Navy—as ferrymen to guide the transport of supplies up and down the coast from Fernandina to Saint Simon's Island.

Earlier in the week, two Union officers from the 4th New Hampshire appear at the front door with a message for Mr. Robert.

"Sir, we have orders for you and your people," states Lieutenant

James Lynch. He stands tall in his crisp, dark-blue frock coat; a light-blue strip runs down his trouser leg to his polished black boots. A single gold bar gleams from his shoulders.

"Since we arrived in Saint Andrew's Sound a few weeks ago, the Confederate forces in East Florida have been deployed to Tennessee. Citizens on the mainland are in a panic. A group of Southern civilians who call themselves regulators have been terrorizing farms and plantations. They are nothing but a group of vigilantes who are taking advantage of the situation. They burn barns and sheds and steal chickens and livestock from both whites and blacks."

Mr. Robert turns to the officer and asks, "What can we do? We have no protection."

"Yes, sir, that brings me to my next point," says Lieutenant Lynch. "I have orders to remove your slaves to Fernandina for their protection."

The last statement sounds like a cannon shot to Mr. Robert. "My slaves! Who's going to farm this plantation?" he asks.

"They will be returned when we can maintain their safety," Lynch assures him. "Keep a few slaves for your needs and your house gardens. I will send a detachment of soldiers to gather the rest and transfer them safely to Fernandina by the week's end." Lynch salutes Mr. Robert.

"In the meantime," warns the other officer, "Keep your eyes open, and report anything unusual to us."

Mr. Robert looks at the soldiers, then out across the plantation. He is fifty-five years old and has never had any trouble on the island. He can't imagine having any trouble now. "Yes, sir, we'll do that," he says. "And thank you for the warning."

Palmetto and saw palm cover the undergrowth, hiding several animals from view. The forest floor is parched. This is a particularly dry summer. A Bermuda High stalls over the southeastern United States, circulating storms to the north. With the exception of an occasional thunderstorm, the island is in the throes of a drought.

Amos looks up over the tackies' bobbing heads and sees a ribbon of

light stretching beneath the canopy. It is dawn. He and Mr. Robert can
see the marsh. All of a sudden, a melody caught in the wind followed
by a deep-voiced harmony punctuates the air.

> If you don't believe I've been redeemed
> God's gonna trouble the water
> I want you to follow him on down to Jordan stream
> (I said) My God's gonna trouble the water
> You know chilly water is dark and cold
> (I know my) God's gonna trouble the water
> You know it chills my body but not my soul
> (I said my) God's gonna trouble the water.

The sounds are at first soft and then gradually rise to a crescendo as
he and Mr. Robert get closer to the marsh. Out on the marsh, six men
with ebony complexions stoop in marsh muck (detritus). They shovel
great gobs of muck into woven reed baskets. It oozes between their toes.
Great beads of sweat roll down their muscular arms. Their shadows race
across the flats. At the edge of the marsh, a long line of oaks and pines
shimmers in the early morning mist.

"This is my best gang," Mr. Robert says to Amos. "Jahmel is the
foreman who has a keen sense of people. He works 'em hard and treats
'em well."

Mr. Robert's slaves haul the muck to the edge of the marsh. They
have only an hour to complete the task. The tide ebbs and flows into the
estuary the marsh supports. It deposits marine life and sediment, which
decomposes and forms a nutrient-rich substance. On the Sea Islands
that hug the southeastern coast, it is used as manure. Mr. Robert uses
it as fertilizer for his cotton crop. Excavating marsh muck is the most
arduous task his slaves perform, and one of the most important. Not
only is it hot, hard work, but sand gnats and marsh insects pepper their
bodies, causing irritating swells. Only slaves of limited capacity and
great strength are used for this operation. Mr. Robert grows Sea Island
cotton, a highly valuable staple, and he is good at it.

"Jahmel!" Mr. Robert yells to the driver. "Get these men off this marsh soon; the tide is coming in fast. Get this muck over to Rayfield, and spread it before noon."

"Yes, sir, Master Robert."

"When you finish that chore, meet me back at the shed," Mr. Robert says. "The Yankees want to move your field hands to Fernandina for their safety. There's trouble over on the mainland. Several folks have been hurt."

One of the slaves catches Amos's eye. He is very dark and stout. Several welts and scars run across his back.

"Master Robert, what happened to that man?"

"Can't say for sure, Amos. I bought him in Charleston a few weeks ago. Those scars on his back are from a severe whipping with a cowskin. His owner wanted to get rid of him. Said he was surly."

Mr. Robert releases his slaves from their morning chores at noon and allows them to return to their quarters. His slaves only work from sunrise until noon. After noon, they tend their own gardens. Tom's family grows summer squash, okra, and turnip greens. Many keep chickens and hogs. They also fish and collect oysters from the estuaries and marshes on the island. Successful slaves sell their produce at the store near the Dungeness plantation or across the sound in Saint Mary's.

A light breeze kicks up off Cumberland Sound and gently cools Mr. Robert and Amos. Busy directing the slaves, they do not see a brace of brown pelicans fly overhead. Quickly, the slaves drag their full baskets off the marsh and load them into the waiting wagons. Long, black ruts fill with water, as the incoming tide slowly spreads over the flats and covers the area they've left only minutes before. Seeking a brief respite from the rising temperatures, Amos and Mr. Robert head for the shade of the maritime forest. Sunlight splinters the forest like dancing fire flies in the early evening.

The allées of trees arch the work road that leads toward the Rayfield tract. Amos watches the field hands head to the fields behind the wagons pulled by a team of strong oxen. They will soon stop at the spring to drink. The island sits on an ancient aquifer and is inundated with natural springs and freshwater sloughs. Both men and mammals look forward to its cool nourishment. Deer and raccoons eagerly drink from the sloughs early in the morning and just before dusk.

Planting is a precarious occupation because rain is unpredictable. Some years the rain irrigates the crops perfectly, providing income and prosperity. In other years, a late rain will destroy cotton as it rots in the fields, and sow economic destruction and foreclosure. All of the slave communities collect rain in large cisterns scattered over the island.

"Master Robert," Amos murmurs. "I've been thinking since the soldiers came a few days ago ... about the warning."

"Yes, Amos," replies Mr. Robert. "Me as well."

"What's going to happen to Tom and his family?" Amos asks.

"They will go to Fernandina with the rest of the field hands. Lieutenant Lynch assures me they will be safe."

"Can Tom stay on the island? He's a good gardener. He takes care of his family's garden." Amos is pleading.

Mr. Robert thinks for a moment, calculating the odds of actually being attacked on the island. He knows the boys are best friends. "I think it will be safe enough here. Tom can care for my garden. He can stay."

Amos is overjoyed. But his mind is still troubled. "Why would people burn and steal from their people?" he asks

"Because they hate ... that's all ... just hate. They hate their lives, they hate other people ... Perhaps they feel life hasn't treated them fairly ... All I know is that they just hate. I am worried, because even though they don't know us, they still hate us ... for what we have."

The fires that burned during the invasion of Fernandina flash back into Amos's mind. He remembers how the flames licked the night sky, like the tongues of wolves eyeing their prey. And he hears the terror in the voices of refugees fleeing over the bridge to safety. Those people were innocent victims of a situation not of their making.

Amos thinks about this for some time as he drives Mr. Robert back to Planter's House. He has never known hate. It is hard for him to imagine how one could hate. But in the near future Amos will also learn to hate. A loud crash interrupts his thoughts. Two doe jump across the road in front of the team and startle them. Amos yells, "Whoa!" He pulls tightly on the reins.

"Good job, lad!" compliments Mr. Robert. "Your quick thinking probably saved us from a mishap. I'm not as young as I used to be. I wouldn't want to be laid up with broken bones."

Amos is proud that he is able to control the team and protect Mr. Robert. This is why Mr. Robert selected him several years ago. He is tall and strong for his age and, according to Mr. Robert, shows intelligence and a great deal of common sense.

They enter the property; a long tabby wall stretches before them. Mr. Robert's slaves built the wall years ago. They collected oyster shells from the middens left by the early Timacua Indians. Old Jake recently told Amos, Amelia, and Tom the story of the Timacua Indians who lived on Cumberland Island for more than four thousand years. Among the staples of their diet were oysters, rich in protein. After eating them, they threw the shells into communal shell mounds, basically trash heaps. After four thousand years, there were a lot of shells to make tabby. Amos is amazed at how many shells were discarded by those early peoples. The slaves excavate the shells; add lime, sand, and saltwater; and mix it together. When it dries, it forms a substance similar to concrete. Many dwellings on the island are constructed from tabby.

Amos pulls the buggy close to the door, and Mr. Robert slowly steps down and walks toward the veranda. "Amos, I've got some accounts to settle in my study. What are you going to do?" he asks.

"Later, when the sun begins to drop and it's not so hot, I'm going fishing up at Big Pond with Tom. Whatever we catch we'll take home to Mom," Amos replies.

"You be careful of the 'gators up there."

"Yes, sir, Master Robert."

Amos runs across the road and toward the slave quarters, where Tom's family lives. He passes several clean, red-brick quarters with tall, red-brick chimneys. Mr. Robert inspects his slave quarters each Sunday, inside and out.

"Tom!" he yells.

"Hey Amos, over here!"

"Ready to go?"

Tom, cinnamon colored and with a big smile, is a bit smaller than Amos. He leans his hoe against the fence. "I just finished hoeing and weeding the vegetable garden Dad planted a few months ago," he says.

Mr. Robert's slaves each have a garden to supplement their diet of pork and corn. Tom's family grows turnips, peas, sweet potatoes. Turnips are high in iron and vitamins and prevent all sorts of deficiencies. Peas are high in protein, and sweet potatoes are rich in several nutrients and vitamins. Tom wears heavy cotton britches covered with dust. Barefoot and shirtless, he grabs two fishing poles, and calls out.

"Let's go! Which way? The road or the river trail?"

"Let's take the river trail," Amos says. "There will be a breeze coming off the sound. It will keep us cool, and we can watch the Union ships patrolling."

Amos and Tom break out onto the river trail and head for Big Pond, fishing poles in hand. From a small bluff, the boys watch the naval activity. Ships, large and small, newly built steamships, smoke billowing from their stacks, slowly slide past. The boys' favorites are the schooners with tall masts and sails that reach for the sky like lonely church spires. They see sailors in blue and white uniforms moving up and down the rigging and setting or unfurling the massive canvas sheets that push the ships to all parts of the world. This flotilla is part of the blockade from Charleston to Savannah to Saint Mary's. The Union Navy's role is to prevent any Southern ship from getting its produce to England and thus financing the Confederate war effort.

"In spite of the blockade," Mr. Robert had said, "blockade runners skillfully elude the Union Navy and get their wares to Nassau, Bermuda, and Havana. On foggy nights, small, fast Confederate vessels slip past the Yankees through the Inland Passage and Saint Mary's outlet. It's a highly profitable venture."

For a moment, Amos wonders, *How does Mr. Robert know this?*

The air briefly blackens as a flock of canvasback ducks drop from the sky. They skim low, hugging the shoreline, looking to set down and feed in the marsh grasses.

"Wait until fall when the weather turns cool," says Amos. "We'll come back and shoot those ducks. Master Robert says I'm old enough to hunt."

"Okay!" Tom replies, "But today we need to catch some big catfish or bass."

Big Pond is a freshwater pond. It is in a dense forest of deciduous and conifer trees. Myrtle, gum, and live oak mingle with yellow and loblolly pine. This blend creates a kaleidoscope of shapes, sizes, and colors. Duckweed, water lilies and spatter dock extend into the pond from the shore like an old shoe tongue. Among the lily pads, yellow lotuses, with their large yellow flowers, look like ballerinas performing on a stage as smooth as the water in the pond. Catfish and bass swim warily beneath the surface, along with freshwater turtles, eels, and alligators.

Amos and Tom love to fish. When they are six years old, they start roaming all over the island in search of the best fishing spot. On the Atlantic side, the waves crash before them as they toss their lines to catch mullet. They stand side by side below the tidal wrack on the long white strip of beach, whiling away long summer afternoons. Together they walk through rose mallow with its tall stems and beautiful pink and white hibiscus flowers. At low tide, they pick oysters on the marsh flats and toss them into woven rush baskets. On the south side of the island, they haul in three-foot sand sharks from Saint Andrew's Sound as they watch dolphins and manatees surface and dive in the ocean. But Big Pond is their favorite spot. They catch more fish there than anywhere else on the island.

Today, as they approach the pond, they see an elegant white-plumed egret on one leg admiring his reflection. Cypress roots that look like elephant toes hold the world down, and textured-bark cypress branches hold up the sky. Tom touches Amos's arm and points to nine turtles sunning themselves on a log. As soon as the boys step to the edge of the pond, the turtles, one by one, peel off the log and slide into the water.

"Let's cast our lines here," Amos suggests.

"Not a bad spot," agrees Tom.

They cast their lines and wait patiently. Though they are still, the air is not. A cacophony of sound breaks the silence of the pond, like the string section of an orchestra warming up: flit, buzz, and hum. Flying insects of all colors and sizes zig and zag over the rich brown surface. Whomp! A great splash as a bass breaks the surface and snags a dragonfly. Concentric ripples flow from the center of the pond and pinpoint its exact location.

Amos and Tom catch several catfish, which they string on a line and leave in the water to keep fresh.

"We've caught enough catfish," Tom says eventually.

"Let's try that spot over there," Amos says.

"Okay! Maybe we'll catch a bass or two," Tom says.

Amos and Tom slowly take their lines from the water. The light is beginning to fade. Ominous shadows dance across the pond. The descending sun creates an impressionistic palette of reds, pinks, and yellow, which bleed into darker hues of blues on the flat water. It is as though a painter has methodically overlaid color after color. On this watery palette, two wood ducks lazily paddle, pushing furrows into the water and leaving a rippled wake in their path.

Just as Amos and Tom step away from the edge of the pond, they hear a crackle off to their right. They peer through the Carolina willow and spikerush, looking for whatever made the noise that raises the hairs on their necks. It came from the dense underbrush.

"Don't move!" Amos whispers to Tom. "Shh ... It is a snake." It slowly slithers toward them, getting closer. "It's coming this way." The brown dry leaves crackle under its weight. "Don't move till we know what it is," he says.

"It's a rattler!" cries Tom.

Indeed it is. Amos soon sees it. Brown and gray diamond patterns slowly move in the understory. Yellow eyes flash in the setting sun as the timber rattler lifts its head to see its prey—perhaps a mouse or a small squirrel. Its poisonous tongue flickers like a horse swishing its tail at horseflies. The boys stand still as sentinels. Their hearts beat fast. Their mouths are as dry as cotton. Beads of sweat boil on their foreheads. Tom's fists grow clammy with fear.

Wham! Suddenly, the snake twists, rolls, and snaps its tail. It struggles. It flashes its fangs and with a whimper of its last rattle, it lies dead. A fishing pole pins its neck to the ground. Just as it is about to strike, Amos skewers it.

By now the sky is dark. The trip back will be difficult. "The light is better on the river trail," Amos says.

Both boys grab the few fish they have caught, their poles, and the snake and strike out toward the trail. The golden light of the sunset illuminates the rippled waters of the sound one last moment before the shades of night are drawn. Darkness rushes in. The moon rises and casts reflected light across the sound. Amos grabs Tom's arm.

"What's that noise? Can you hear it?"

"No," Tom says.

"It's coming from the water," Amos says.

They are on a bluff overlooking the salt marsh and the sound. Amos and Tom crouch behind a large gum tree and hide in the shadows. Now, they both hear it—oars splashing not too far away. Someone is rowing a boat toward them.

Amos quietly says, "They're not good oarsmen. Too much splashing."

"Who would row a boat here this time of night?" Tom asks. "Think it's anybody we know? Do you suppose they're Yankees?"

"I doubt it, Tom," says Amos. "Let's get back and tell Master Robert."

5

Fire

Amos and Tom drop their fishing poles, the fish, and the dead rattler. "Come on," Amos whispers. "Let's get out of here!"

The boys sprint down the river trail to alert Mr. Robert. Tom steps on a dead limb; the snapping sound startles an owl, which screeches as it swoops from its high perch. The silver moon lights its way like silken ribbons through the branches. Amos and Tom find their way easily; this is a path they've traveled a hundred times.

Dark shadows stretch across the path like a haint's long fingers. Haints make Tom so nervous, he bites his lower lip. Like many slaves living on the coastal islands, he is superstitious. Since he was a small child, the older people have told him stories about haints. What worries him most is that all the stories end with someone's death.

His imagination runs riot. A squirrel rustling in the leaves or a family of raccoons scrambling up a tree sends shivers up his spine. Splinters of light or a reflection through the leaves terrify him. He remembers a story his grandmother told him:

> A long time ago on the island, up at the old Reeves' place, a driver and a slave got into a terrible argument late one afternoon. The driver grabbed a cowskin and laid several large welts across the slave's back to control him. That night the slave, seething with anger, went to a woodshed

and grabbed an axe. He calmly walked over to the driver's quarters and knocked on the door. When the door opened, the slave pushed the driver back in to the room and viciously hacked him to death, leaving his body in a pool of blood on the floor. Quietly, he left by the backdoor. In the years that followed, strange lights were often seen at the driver's house. When darkness smothered the island like a black glove, a bright ball of light would appear on the doorstep. It would then enter the house and leave through the backdoor, perhaps looking for the slave who committed the murder.

Tom's worst fear is the haints that wait in trees at night. Hungry, they devour the body of any unsuspecting traveler. His grandmother's stories include one about a slave who wanted to visit a friend at a nearby plantation one afternoon. Unfortunately, he made the mistake of leaving his village too late. As dusk settled, he went through the woods, thinking he would save time. The next day his clothes were found beneath a large oak tree. He was never seen again.

Amos tells Tom not to worry; there are no haints. Those stories are intended to keep young children from straying into the woods and getting lost.

"No, Amos, that's not true," Tom says. "Haints exist. I know it."

Finally, they stop at the edge of a clearing. The lantana, bitterweed, and broomsedge seed themselves and grow along the edge of Stafford Field. Once a forest of live oak, the field now grows a variety of crops, including cotton, corn, and peas. The moon rising in the east offers enough light to see across the field. Amos and Tom quickly spot Planter's House. Moonlight reflects off the roof and illuminates the tall chimneys. To the right, a single beam of light stretches like a beacon toward the boys from a downstairs window. To the left, barely visible, twelve slave cabins huddle against a bank of trees. Since the rising and setting sun govern the slaves' lives, no lights are visible in the cabins.

"Master Robert! Master Robert!" Amos calls as his bare feet pound across the veranda. He raps on the massive door. In a few minutes, it opens slowly. Old James, Mr. Robert's butler, peers out.

"Who is it?"

"It's me! Amos! James, get Master Robert!"

"I'm here."

Mr. Robert stands in the glow of the lamp, his shoulders slightly stooped. The soft light washes his face and highlights his gray hair and eyes. He looks old and tired.

"What is it, Amos?" he asks nervously.

"Master Robert, Tom and I saw some men, maybe five or six, in a boat trying to land not far from here, " he spits out breathlessly.

"Where?"

"Up at Table Point," Amos says.

"Did they have guns?" Mr. Robert asks.

"We don't know!" says Tom.

"It was dark!" Amos says at the same time.

Mr. Robert is tense. "Come with me out to the veranda," he says. He looks toward the dark forest and the main road that leads into it. This road runs the entire length of the island. It carries cotton and produce to the landings for shipment. It allows slaves to travel quickly from one place to another on the island.

"If they come tonight, it will be down that road," Mr. Robert says. "We don't have any protection. We need to get help from the Yankees. Tom, run home and tell your family to warn your people, and go hide in the woods. Amos, run to the dock, take one of the small boats, and row over to the sloop, the one called *Pawnee*. Tell Commander Drayton about our troubles. Tell him we need troops with guns!

"Now, get!" commands Mr. Robert. "Maybe luck will be with us, those ruffians might head for the old Shaw place."

In his excitement, he loses his train of thought. He recently purchased the Shaw tract. It is now his. Approximately four hundred bales of cotton are stored in a shed, waiting for an opportune time to sell. There are barns, sheds, about 250 head of cattle, as well as hogs, which roam freely, chickens, and equipment. All in all, this is an expensive piece of property. If it is destroyed, it will mean economic hardship for Mr. Robert.

Amos runs to the dock, unties the mooring line, jumps in the boat, sets the oar pins, and rows furiously toward the Union fleet. The night is calm. A gentle breeze carries the scent of food cooking from the fleet. The tide favors his voyage. A dolphin crosses his bow; then two more. Three playful dolphins dive and break the surface, unaware of his plight. He pulls hard and fast. *Will I get back in time? Who are those men and what do they want?*

Amos hears the spars creak and smells the tar from the lines and rigging. The sounds of the waves lapping against the sloop's hull tell him he is close. All of a sudden, a shout rings in the darkness.

"Who goes there?" booms a voice from the bow.

Amos looks into the sights of a gun bearing down on him. A Union sentry watches him warily as he comes along side of the *Pawnee*.

"Throw me a line! We need help!" yells Amos. He is pulled aboard and taken immediately to Commander Drayton.

"Commander Drayton, Master Robert is in trouble," he explains quickly. "A group of armed men from the mainland just came ashore."

Commander Drayton knows Mr. Robert. Through their business contacts, they have become friends. He purchases livestock and vegetables from Mr. Robert's plantation. Mr. Robert also leases his slaves to serve as ferrymen for the Union Navy. When Commander Drayton realizes the men the boys saw might be regulators, he orders a detachment to row back across the sound with Amos. Not only might Mr. Robert be in trouble, but any damage or harm done to his plantation will affect the Union Navy as well. Eight soldiers from the 4th New Hampshire Regiment board a skiff and row toward the dock. They are armed with new Springfield rifles and looking for a fight.

The moon that provided light earlier begins to set, and the shoreline is difficult to see. Soon they reach the dock, tie off their boats, and climb up on the dock. The detachment quickly forms into a line of twos and, in military fashion, jogs in double step toward Planter's House.

When the regulators land, they tie their boat in the cordgrass, just a few steps from where Amos and Tom first saw them.

"Where are we going?" asks one of the men.

"Follow me," says Nathaniel Wilkes, their leader. "There is a cotton shed not too far from here I want to burn."

A year earlier, Wilkes had rowed to the island under the cover of darkness. He knew the island supported a large deer population, and he hadn't eaten for a few days. *A venison roast would taste mighty good about now*, he thought to himself. He landed his boat at Table Point and hid it in the reeds. He climbed onto the bank, shouldered his musket, and quietly crept to a large field at the edge of a forest, where large herds of deer were grazing. At dusk, fat does left the shelter of the forest first and moved into the meadow. When it is safe, a buck or two followed the herd. Wilkes knew he would have an easy shot. He waited, patiently. Soon out of the darkness, he saw the herd move toward him. Slowly, he raised his musket, took aim, and squeezed the trigger. The loud noise startled the other deer. They bounded away, waving their tails like white flags into the safety of the woods. He pulled his knife from his belt to gut the fat doe. A shot rang out. He'd been spotted. Quickly, he ran for his boat.

He hasn't forgotten being shot at a year earlier by one of Mr. Robert's servants, who caught him poaching deer. "I want to burn that old buck's cotton barn," he says. "He took food from my mouth; now I'll take food from his."

A poor white, Nathaniel Wilkes owns no property and has no respect for other people's property. He has had many brushes with the law. The list of offenses is as long as his musket barrel, and he is a regular visitor to the Saint Mary's courthouse and jail, charged with assault, domestic violence, and the mistreatment of animals. Two of his yellow, tobacco-stained teeth are missing. Disturbing the peace and brawling are typical of the complaints lodged against him.

When the state of Georgia appeals to the patriotism of its young men, Wilkes and his cohorts turn a deaf ear, although most Georgians rush enthusiastically to sign up. The Confederacy conscripts her finest men. Left behind are old men, young boys, and social misfits. Wilkes and his band of ruffians take advantage of the situation and prey upon defenseless families. They pillage, burn, and steal anything and everything in their path. South Georgia descends into a Hobbesian society, and Wilkes becomes a leader in a lawless land.

They light torches and cut through saw palm and palmetto in the understory to reach the main road. The venom in Wilkes's blood poisons his mind. He is just one step above slaves and freed men on the social ladder; his social position is precarious at best. Years of grinding poverty have taken its toll. Now he has a chance to get back at the ones he believes keep him down. Tonight, he will vindicate those perceived wrongs by burning Mr. Robert's property and in the process perhaps steal a few chickens and livestock.

"This should be easy as collecting eggs. Nobody knows we are here," he says.

"The moon is low in the sky," says one of the others. "That will give us cover when we escape."

Five men, poorly clad in grimy homespun, emerge from the understory and turn to the road. Two of them are barefoot. Unwashed for several days, their hair is greasy and tangled. Each carries a pistol tucked under his belt. Wilkes throws an old musket over his shoulder, the one he used to poach the deer. He kicks up some dirt and spits a huge glob of tobacco on the ground.

"Let's go. The shed is about a quarter mile from here. We going to have some fun tonight," he muses.

Amos and the soldiers rush to Mr. Robert. He is still on the veranda, looking toward the road into the forest. Tom too has returned. He has warned the slaves, and they are hiding in the woods. Amos notices that the sky above the tree line is brightly lit with stars. He is a sky watcher. The rotation of the constellations fascinates him. Sometimes at night, out in the large field, Amos lies on his back and speculates about Orion, who hunts in the southern sky. In many ways the stars are his friends. Throughout the summer he measures the progress of the Big Dipper, which will soon become a guiding beacon for slaves following the

Underground Railroad. Tonight, it guides them as well. Recalling the star of Bethlehem, it sits directly over the Shaw cotton shed.

"Sir, where is your property?" a soldier asks.

"Follow that road for a about a half a mile. You will see it on the left." Mr. Robert points his finger in the right direction.

"Let's move!" The eight Union soldiers resume their jog. Amos runs to the carriage shed and hooks up one of the tackies to Mr. Robert's buggy. He snaps the whip and takes it to the veranda. Mr. Robert jumps in.

"Tom, you jump in the back," says Mr. Robert. "Follow the soldiers, Amos! We don't have much time!"

The sky above is bright, but darkness closes in as soon as they enter the forest. Amos's eyes are slow to adjust to night vision; he has trouble seeing. The moon has set, and little light is visible. The canopy that arches over the road prevents the bright lights of the Milky Way Galaxy from guiding their way. The buggy is surrounded by darkness. It is as if an octopus squirted a black jet of ink around them, a miasma that engulfs every object, human and non-human, in its wake.

Wilkes and his group of regulators spot the cotton shed. Excited, they turn off the main road and walk toward it. They ignite a torch made from dried saw palm. It burns brightly. The livestock, uneasy about the smell of strangers, begin to moan. Chickens, ducks, and geese cluck, quack, and honk. As the men approach the shed, the poultry scatter in all directions.

"Don't just stand there. Grab a few chickens while we are here," Wilkes orders. "They'll taste good later on."

Three of Wilkes's men chase the chickens. The chickens flap their wings and scatter everywhere. The men try to corner them against the shed, and feathers fly as the chickens dart to outmaneuver these unwanted guests. Wilkes looks at the cattle, which are all lined up, looking back at him. *Too large to take in the boat*, he thinks. *I'll come back later*. The chickens escape and run into the woods and safety. In the confusion, Wilkes's men are separated.

The foliage slowly changes as the buggy bumps over the road, heading north toward the cotton shed. Sheets of Spanish moss listlessly hanging from the live oak contrast with the tall straight stands of loblolly pine. For the first time since they've been on the road, Amos can see far enough to detect the faint outline of the soldiers. In a few minutes, they will reach the edge of the pine grove and cross the field into the Shaw property.

"We are here!" announces Mr. Robert, as the soldiers turn left and move off the road. "They'll be at the shed soon."

All of a sudden, the air is filled with reports of Springfield rifles. Several cracks of small arms followed by the loud boom of a musket signal the beginning of a skirmish. Amos and Tom are about to witness their first military action on the island. Like a scene in a novel, it unfolds before them. A pink glow like an early morning sunrise catches Amos's attention.

"They torched the shed!" exclaims Mr. Robert.

The flames race through the shed, driven by the west wind coming off the sound. The fire creates enough light to see a group of Union soldiers down on one knee, tightly packed, and shooting into the woods behind the inferno. They pin down Nathaniel Wilkes and his band of regulators with the rapid firing of their new Springfield rifles.

The acrid smell of smoke from the cotton and wood permeates Amos's nose. White flecks of cinders rain down on Mr. Robert, Tom, and Amos like a spring snowstorm.

"Amos, move the buggy away from those cinders," orders Mr. Robert. "We don't need to get burned."

As Amos pulls the reigns and turns the tackie to avoid the heat and flames, he notices small patches of fire igniting the field. The hot summer with little rain has dried out the hackenberry and bracken. The greatest threat to planters on Cumberland Island during the summer months are the many lightning strikes, which ignite the tinder-dry saw palm and palmetto in the understory. The heat from the quick burn releases seeds from the pine cones, which can lie dormant on the ground for up to eight years. This is nature's way of ensuring a healthy pine forest. But sometimes the fires burn uncontrolled and destroy property as well. Tonight the fire is started by humans who care for neither life nor property. Flames fanned by the wind crackle the dry grasses. The night air, porous as a sponge, is soon filled with deafening sounds—of orders, gunshots, cattle, poultry, burning property, and destruction. The beef cattle grow increasingly nervous; finally, they bolt and stampede between the formation of soldiers and the woods from where the Wilkes gang is shooting.

"Get out of the way!" the squad leader yells.

"Get out of here!" Wilkes yells to his men, who have been surprised by the Yankee soldiers. This is their chance to escape. They split up and flee deeper into the woods. Behind them, they leave a major conflagration. The flames lick high into the air.

"Put out the grass fire," orders the squad leader.

The soldiers quickly reorganize. The regulators, at least for the moment, have escaped. The cattle huddle at the end of the field that is now in flames; they watch like witnesses at a crime scene. The soldiers' attention turns to putting out the blaze. Amos and Tom jump from Mr. Robert's buggy, tie it to a tree on the edge of the field, and run to help the soldiers put out the fire. A small outbuilding filled with shovels, tynes, and rakes provides the firefighting tools everyone needs. The flames rapidly creep toward the main road. Snakes, insects, and small field mice slither, hop, and run as they try to escape a fiery death. A mother hog and nine piglets squeal as the flames warm the bristles on their backs.

The fire has to be stopped at the road, or Mr. Robert will suffer a major disaster. Across the road, several hundred acres of hay, dry as a bone, and a number of buildings storing equipment and animals are in peril. If the flames jump the road, everything in their wake will burn. Mr. Robert, too old to fight a fire of this magnitude, anxiously watches from his seat on the buggy.

Armed with rakes and shovels, the small contingent of fire fighters relentlessly attacks the flames. Fortunately, the wind shifts and blows in from the east, causing the fire to burn back on and extinguish itself. The cotton shed continues to burn brightly in the night. Flames quickly burn through the roof, sending shingles up into the night air.

A great loud crash thunders through the night when the roof collapses. A shower of sparks and cinders rise high like fireworks on the Fourth of July.

From his perch on the buggy, Mr. Robert witnesses the barn slowly burn to the ground. Only the large poles that framed it stand, like the black pistils of a flower mourning death. The cotton smolders for several days. The smoke is seen all over the island and as far away as Saint Mary's.

The chaos and confusion of the fire and the shooting separates not only the gang, but the soldiers and Amos and Tom as well. The night is dark, and shadows from the flames dance across the wall of trees leading in to the forest. All eyes and energy are on the fire, which draws attention away from Wilkes. He and his gang escape into the forest, but where? Much of the field between the cotton shed and the road still burns brightly. Hot, black ashes reach to the edge of the woods. Barefoot, Tom and Amos skirt the edge of the woods to get back to Mr. Robert. The light from the fire dilates their eyes so they lose their night vision. They cannot see into the forest.

"Yeow!" Tom screams. "A haint … a haint's got me, got me round my neck!"

Amos turns quickly. A man has Tom by his neck. Veins protrude from his scrawny arms. His eyes, set on either side of a dislocated nose, burn black in the light of the fire. Tom smells his foul breath and the stench from his clothing. He feels the heat from the man's body, as a pistol pushes into the back of his neck.

"You tell them Yankee boys to put their weapons down, or I'll shoot you."

Tom trembles with fear. "Do what he says, Amos."

The regulator tightens his grip around Tom's neck and pulls him back into the woods away from the light.

"Get help, Amos!" Tom yells. "Don't let him kill me."

Amos runs to the squad leader. "They got Tom!" he screams.

The soldiers turn and peer into the woods. They had dropped their Springfields on the ground to fight the fire. They can't see a thing, but they hear the regulator yell to his men.

"Y'all get over here! I got me a nigger boy. He's going to be our ticket out of here. Hey! You Yankee boys walk away from your weapons. or the boy gets it."

The understory rings with the sound of crackling leaves, as if three deer have bolted. Amos hears the snap of dry branches. He hears the regulators cuss as their bodies are slashed by the razor-sharp tips of saw palmetto and they brush against the thorns of the devil's walking stick. The understory is shelter and protection for many animals. But for humans it is a gauntlet that can shred a man's clothes in a matter of minutes.

"The damn cracker's got the kid!" Nathaniel Wilkes is giddy. For the first time in his life, he is in control. He is in charge. He is dripping with the power of the powerless. He has eight Yankees at bay, unarmed. He's burned Mr. Robert's cotton shed, which was worth an unimaginable amount of money. He revels in his revenge. And despite the chaos unleashed by the fire and the surprise presence of the Yankee troops, he has a hostage to ensure his escape.

"Make sure the nigger doesn't get away," he orders. "Let's get back to the boat."

Wilkes and his men push Tom ahead of them as they walk through the charred field and return to the road. Wilkes is last in line and backs away, covering his men with the musket. No one else moves. The soldiers watch them escape in frustration. In a few minutes, Wilkes will row his boat back to Saint Mary's and plunder another defenseless farm.

What are they going to do with Tom? Amos wonders. Once they are in the water they will have no need for him.

Mr. Robert watches this scene unfold from his buggy. The regulators do not know he is there. Their attention has been focused on chasing chickens and burning the cotton shed. When the soldiers began shooting, Mr. Robert was still on the main road, and the regulators did not see him. And he is angry. No words can describe his rage. He had seen his shed burned, cattle stampeded, and had the fire not been stopped at the road, he would have lost several more fields in cultivation. And now his property, on e of his few remaining slaves is being held hostage and is in grave danger.

He reaches under the buggy seat and pulls out a new Springfield Model 1855 rifled musket that Commander Drayton gave him for protection.

"Robert, someday you might need to use this new musket," Drayton said. "It is rifled, which makes it extremely accurate at long distances. Unlike the smooth bore muskets, which can kill a man at about fifty yards, this one is good for up to five hundred yards."

"Thank you, sir," Mr. Robert said. "I love to hunt and can shoot very well. But I don't think I will be shooting at people on this island."

"Well, I hope not. But a lot is happening on the mainland that makes me nervous," the commander said. "Hopefully, you won't have to use it.".

Mr. Robert carefully slides off the buggy, trying not to make any noise that might alert Wilkes to his presence, and quietly steals into the shadows of the woods, unseen. From this vantage point, he considers his next move. *Intercept them on the road?* The five men are both desperate and dangerous, and Tom is their shield. Between them they have four side arms and a musket; that he is sure of, but perhaps they have more. *Not a good plan*, he thinks. It is still dark, and he has the element of surprise. If he can get behind them, they will not know how many men might be with him. A third option flashes into his mind.

> If I can get to the boat before them, I can save Tom. I know every inch of this island. I have purchased tract after tract, cultivated acres of cotton, and hunted and fished here all my life.

His thoughts flow as he plans.

> I have walked, inspected, surveyed, and supervised all the areas of the island, from the pristine strip of the eighteen-mile beach on the east side to the freshwater sloughs and Big Pond to the west. I have pulled oysters at low tide in the marshes and supervised field hands excavating muck for the cotton fields. I have roped tackies and sold them in Saint Mary's and cut timber for buildings and firewood.

It is true. He knows the island. Now, he needs to use that knowledge to save Tom.

Meanwhile, Wilkes and his gang, intent on escaping, follow the main road to avoid the perils of the understory. But it means they must walk a longer distance to get back to the boat.

I'll cut through the understory, Mr. Robert thinks. *I will follow a deer trail.* Generations of deer and all animals have worn down a path that is easy to follow and is clear of the brambles and thorns of the understory. Wilkes and his gang will not expect this. The dark night conceals his movements in the shadows of the tall trees. His anger burns as well.

A murmur softly wafts in from the sound. He listens intently. It is the gentle lapping of waves. He reaches the river trail. He aims to cut off Wilkes at Table Point before he can row away. The stars light his way. He reaches a small bluff that overlooks the sound and sees a small boat barely hidden in the reeds.

He stands as silent as a sentinel, listening. He does not make a sound. Mr. Robert checks his rifle. It is loaded. He slips down the bank and steps into the water. Reaching for his knife, he cuts the line. The boat slowly drifts away from the island, carried by the current.

He climbs the bank and hides in a thicket behind a gum tree, the same tree Amos and Tom used for cover earlier. From this vantage point, he achieves superiority. He is above his enemies, has a clear field of vision, and is hidden. He waits, coiled like a rattler ready to strike.

Off to his right, he hears voices.

"Where's the boat?" yells Wilkes.

"I thought we left it here."

"Split up, and find it. We don't have much time. The Yankees will be on us soon."

Mr. Robert's plan works. The five men separate to look for the boat. Two walk north along the bank, and two more search the reeds to the south. The last still has Tom. He raises his rifle and aims down the sight at Wilkes. Though it is still dark, Wilkes's musket identifies him.

"Let the boy go, and drop your weapons," Mr. Robert commands

Wilkes immediately turns toward the sound and fires his musket.

A loud boom splits the air. Smoke billows from the barrel; a mini ball ricochets off a tree close to Mr. Robert. He knows that is Wilkes's last shot. He draws a breath, takes careful aim, and squeezes the trigger. The mini ball spins from the barrel and finds its mark. Mr. Robert shatters Wilkes's shoulder, and he collapses in the water. His blood reddens the water in the reeds. The others search in vain for Mr. Robert. He is well concealed. They cannot see him. In fear for their lives, they drop their weapons.

"Tom, get over here!"

6

Live Oak

Long shadows stretched across the beach as the sun set behind the oaks and pines of the maritime forest. Amos, Amelia, and Tom walk on the beach. They are collecting lettered olive shells and sand dollars. Shadows from the dunes—small, windblown hills of sand that eventually become large hills of sand—create a mural of mountains on the beach. They have never seen a mountain or even a hill over forty feet high, but they walk the shadow line up and down the beach. The coastal islands lie low and flat in the water. Barefooted, they feel the hard, packed wet sand beneath their feet; it feels like a washboard and cools their toes. Rivulets of water from the early tide flow to the sea. Sand pipers and terns share the beach and race with each other along the water's edge. Every few steps, a brace of terns flies into the air, like leaves blowing in autumn. Sea gulls and black skimmers screech over the roar and crash of the waves that pound the beach. Amelia, Amos, and Tom play tag with the waves. First, they run fast toward the receding water and then they run hastily back, as fast as they can, away from the incoming waves.

"Let's cut through the forest and save a few steps," Amos suggests.

"Yeah!" says Tom.

"The canopy will keep us cool," says Amelia.

They race from the beach, jump over the wrack debris that has washed ashore after violent storms, and head straight toward the dune system, created by the persistent east wind. On the top of each dune are large clumps of sea oats, which anchor the dunes with long roots to the ground. The windswept sand engulfs everything in its path. At one time a stand of trees offered shade to the surrounding area. Now, strangled by the sand, it is a ghost forest, its mummified trees, dry, cracked, and gray, seem to march like weary soldiers toward the sea.

Amos, Amelia, and Tom run quickly through this section of the dunes, jumping over the salt-meadow cordgrass and avoiding the sandspur; they have accidently stepped on its sharp painful burr many times before. The sand feels like a hot plate beneath their feet. They soon reach the freshwater slough that lies between the trees and the dunes and dip their feet in the water. It cools their feet. In the early morning and late afternoon deer, raccoon and bobcat drink from these sloughs.

"Let's get a drink here," Tom yells. "I'm thirsty!"

"Me too," replies Amelia.

After they've had enough to drink, they venture into the maritime forest. Shadows, long as tall ship masts, stretch across the under canopy. Sweet gum, water oak, and sycamore trees fill the forest. Long vines climb from the ground to the highest branches of the hickory and magnolia trees. Squirrels run up and down the vines and scold the three intruders. Soon, it gets dark, and Tom and Amelia grow anxious.

"Watch out for the witches in the woods," Tom cautions.

"Oh! The haints, those haints, will wrap their long, bony fingers around your neck and snatch you into a big ole bag," Amelia agrees.

"Stop that nonsense!" Amos says. "There ain't no haints or witches that want you two." He laughs.

The maritime forest is alive with sound. The thunk-thunk-thunk of a pileated woodpecker searching for insects on a laurel oak catches their attention.

"Oh, mister woodpecker, he just makes a racket drilling for insects. I bet he keeps them haints and witches up late at night." Amos chuckles to himself.

All of a sudden, Tom gives out a yelp. "Oh, my toe, I think I broke my toe!" he yells. "I tripped on something … it is big and hard."

They look down and see a large wooden template, a mould for makin ga piece to a ship buried like a treasure chest. Almost hidden, it is covered in leaves and ground cover. They wonder what it is.

"I've never seen anything like it." Tom says. "It is some type of tool, I think."

"Old Jake will know what it is," says Amos. "He is a mechanic and knows everything about machinery. He can tell us what it is."

During the next few minutes, the threesome uncover the template and realize it is much too heavy to drag to Old Jake's quarters. Not only that, but Tom and Amelia start to worry about the haints and witches who might be hiding in the branches and waiting to snag them by their necks.

"Let's get back home quick!"

Caught up in the excitement, they let down their defenses. As young children, they were taught to be cautious in the forest. One might come upon a rattlesnake basking in the sun, an alligator up a Big Pond, or the most dangerous, a feral wild boar, with sharp tusks made to tear its victim apart. Intent on getting back to Old Jake, not one of them looks up. Overhead a large flock of grizzly turkey vultures soar; they ride the thermals in constant search of food. Turkey vultures have a keen sense of smell, which helps them locate fresh carcasses. Large birds with broad wings and ragged feathers, they are a sinister sight in flight.

"Oh my!" Amelia shrieks. "What is that smell?"

"It's putrid!" Tom exclaims.

The stench almost suffocates them. Never has a smell caused them to choke. Tears well in their eyes.

"What is it?"

Through the glade, they see vultures huddling like homeless men around a fire. Nine or ten are fighting over a deer carcass. Their ugly red heads and sharply hooked beaks tear at the muscle tissue, stretching and fighting over long strings of red meat. Like mad men in a demonic dance, they hop and flap their wings. In a frenzy, they gobble the remains. The heat and humidity decompose the deer rapidly. The vultures soon will strip all the meat from the bones and leave only the skeletal remains.

They run too close to the vultures. Immediately, the birds all take flight in a savage fury. The black horde circles over Amos, Amelia, and Tom. In an instance, one regurgitates his portion of the deer onto Tom.

"They are spitting on me!" he yells.

Amos looks up and see at least thirteen vultures angrily spewing remains at them. Gobs of vomit splat on their heads and cover their hair. First, the stench and now the bombardment of partially digested foul smelling entrails—it is more than they can bear.

"Let's get out of here!" they cry.

Tom forgets about his sore toe and sprints with Amos and Amelia. As fast as they can, they run from the flock of angry vultures.

The three race through the forest until they reach the clearing next to Planter's House and their can see their quarters. The last rays of the sun cast a golden glow over the meadow, which is strewn with hackberry, St. Andrew's cross, and passion flower. Feeling like they are wading in water, they push through the pokeberry and Joe-Pye weed to find Old Jake and see if he knows what they found.

"Mr. Jake, Mr. Jake" they breathlessly yell.

"We found something big in the forest," Amos says. "It looks like a tool of some type. Can you tell us what it is?"

Old Jake slowly opens the door, peers out of his cabin, and sees Amos, Amelia, and Tom. They all speak at once.

"Mr. Jake, when we were crossing through the forest, we found a big wooden block with curves!" says Amos.

"We wanted to show it to you!" says Amelia.

"It is too large to drag back!" says Tom.

"Slow down … you're all talking too fast. Oh, Lordy, what is that smell?"

Tom tells Old Jake about their mishap with the vultures.

"Well you should know by now those ugly birds are territorial," says Old Jake. "You invaded they territory and got punished for it. You're lucky it wasn't a wild boar."

"What do you think it is?" Amelia says.

"Come in, and calm down, but firsat get yourselves washed up. " Old Jake says. "Tell me, where did you find this mysterious object?"

"Not far from the dune meadow," they say in unison.

———∽∾∿———

In 1785, George Washington gives Cumberland Island to General Nathaniel Greene in return for his services during the American Revolution. Greene notes in his journal:

> We visited all the islands particularly Cumberland in which I am interested. I find it a very valuable piece of property and had I funds to improve it to advantage it might be made one of the first commercial objects on the Continent. The island is twenty odd miles long and a great part of it excellent for Indigo. The situation is favorable for trade, the place healthy and prospects delightful. On the seaside there is a beach eighteen miles long and as level as a floor and as hard as a rock. It is the pleasantest ride I ever saw.

Thus begins the Greene-Miller relationship with Cumberland Island. Nathaniel Greene's untimely death in 1786 means he will never see his plans for Cumberland come to fruition. But Catharine Greene, his widow, and her second husband, Phineas Miller, establish residence on the island in May 1800.

"Come, sit by the fireplace," says Old Jake. "This story will take a long time to tell."

Old Jake scuffles over to his favorite chair and slowly sits down. He wears one of Mr. Robert's hand-me-down velvet burgundy jackets. Worn with age, it gives him a look of understated authority.

"Years ago, when I was your age, I worked on the Greene plantation. Master Greene had moved to Cumberland from Mulberry Grove plantation in Savannah. The oppressive heat and yellow fever epidemics convinced him and his wife, Miss Caty, to develop the island. At that time, we didn't grow as much cotton as we do today. Miss Caty grew all sorts of plants and vegetables. She had greenhouses to grow her fruit, especially citrons. After the war, the British bought her citrons to prevent scurvy in the navy. Then a very sad thing happened. Master Greene died of sunstroke one hot afternoon while he was visiting Mulberry Grove plantation. And then things changed."

'What sort of changes?" Amos asks.

"Master Miller, who used to keep books for Master Greene, married Miss Caty and took over the plantation. He knew that the live oak was valuable for building ships. When our country was new, it needed a navy. Master Miller worked out an arrangement with the government to cut enough live oak to build one of the new frigates. At the time though, nobody had any idea how difficult this project would be."

"I can just imagine," Tom says. "Those trees are big and heavy."

"Yes, they are big and heavy. Many of the trees grow between forty and seventy feet high. When I was your age, I saw oaks whose shade would cover half an acre. We have perfect conditions on the island to grow live oak, which tolerates the salt spray from the ocean and can grow in just about any soil condition.

"Well, we couldn't cut the trees ourselves. We didn't have enough skilled labor. Soon lots of men from up North came here. They came in the winter months and built huge logging camps. Master Miller hired Thomas Stafford, Master Robert's father, to oversee the timber operation.

"Miss Caty was determined to build a magnificent home on the island. In fact, I helped build it. First, Master Miller found a level area, where the old mission had been located, to build the new house. It was twenty feet above sea level and was an excellent place for the house and gardens. We dug up the oyster shells in the midden and made tabby for the walls. That building eventually grew four stories high. We poured tabby in wooden forms for the base, which was six feet wide. By the time we reached the roof, it was seventy-six feet from the ground. And the walls were four feet wide. We built an attic and covered the roof in copper.

"The house servants lived in the basement, which also had a cellar for wine and food. Above the basement were twenty rooms, including a reception area with tall windows on the first floor. The second floor contained living quarters for the family, including drawing rooms, a dining room, and parlors. On the third floor, the family had large bedrooms.

"The house faced the north, with a long terrace to catch the cooling breezes. Six Doric pilasters rose from the first floor to the cornices, which gave a commanding impression. The entrance was faced with granite, complemented by four balanced windows and a massive front door. The south side of the house also had four windows facing the marsh. There were four brick chimneys, two on each side of the house, which supported sixteen fireplaces. It was a magnificent house. But it was never completed. Guests often complained about dining on fine furniture and china surrounded by rough tabby, complete with protruding oyster shells.

"We also built many outbuildings for the estate—a three-story cotton ginning house, carpentry and blacksmith's shops, latrines, greenhouses and a very interesting round building called an orangery, used to grow oranges. Miss Caty made lots of money producing crystallized citric acid, which was used to prevent scurvy."

Jake takes a breath, which allows Amos to interrupt and turn the conversation back to the template buried in the woods. "Mr. Jake, did that wooden block we found this afternoon have anything to do with timber cutting?" he asks.

"I believe it did. In fact, I think what you found is an old wooden mold or template the axe men used to finish their work. As Tom said, live oak is very heavy, and extra weight costs money. The sawyers would cut the parts of the tree that they wanted for the ships' ribs, you know, the curved parts. Once cut and on the ground, the sawyer would use the old wooden template to cut the piece exactly right. That way, much of the work was completed before the timber was shipped up north to the shipyards.

"I'm getting ahead of myself. Let me tell about that whole operation," Jake says as he taps some tobacco into the bowl of his pipe. Slowly, he bends forward toward the fire and lights a straw. The flame dances as he puts the piece of straw to his pipe. Curls of smoke soon waft throughout the cabin.

"One cool morning in November, Master Miller sent several of us to the south side of the island to help offload a schooner from New England. I remember he was very excited. 'The cutters are here!' he exclaimed.

"The sky was light in the east, but the sun had not yet risen. Not far off shore a beautiful two-mast schooner sailed toward us. As she came about, we could see the entire ship. The crew tossed anchor lines from both bow and stern. Sails were quickly reefed from the main and mizzen masts.

"The sun slowly rose and cast long shadows that raced toward the shore. A gentle breeze carried the sounds of activity—orders given, oxen bellowing, chickens clucking, and the voices of men carrying out theirduties. We saw two long boats descend from the deck and hit the water with a splash. In a few minutes, a large brown ox hanging by two large straps was lowered into the first boat. Four more oxen were loaded in this fashion.

"I had never seen anything like this in my entire life," Jake remarks. "The idea of sailing oxen from New England had never occurred to me. It was simply amazing. And to this day, I will never forget my first encounter with those Yankees who came to log live oak.

"The crew of the first boat long boat rowed toward us. They floated ashore, gently pushed by spilling breakers, slow moving waves. Early in the morning, the ocean tended to be calm ... sometimes almost flat. Teamsters carrying goad sticks prodded the oxen onto the beach. 'Gee' and 'haw,' they yelled. The oxen moved left or right on command.

"They unloaded not only oxen but also timber carts, tools, cooking pots, and great supplies of food. After they'd stowed the supplies under canvas to keep them dry, the men set up camp. It seemed that everyone had an axe, and they cut poles for the frameworks of their huts. Their huts were large enough to accommodate eight men, a cook, and a young boy who kept the hut clean. Close to each of the fifteen huts was a cookhouse, a store shed, and a covered place for dining. When the frames were erected, the men cut large palmetto leaves, bound them together, and used them for the roof and sides. In a few days, we had over a hundred men and oxen ready to spend the winter cutting live oak.

"Cutting the trees is not only hard work, it is dangerous work," Old

Jake says. "To keep morale high, every attempt was made to serve good food. In fact, the cook in camp was considered the most important person, next to the blacksmith. The men ate dried salt fish, corn meal, Indian corn, dried beans, flour, salt, pepper, molasses, coffee, and tea. To break the monotony of this diet, they were allowed to hunt the hogs that roamed freely on the island, and occasionally cattle from Master Miller's herd were slaughtered.

"Young boys helped the cooks, carried water, chopped wood, and kept the fires going. It was also their job to keep the fires stoked at night so they would not go out. Several times, Master Miller sent me to the camps. The cooks offered me beans cooked in a Dutch oven and a concoction they called hasty pudding. It was a mixture of corn meal, salt, and water mixed into mush. I also ate bread fried in lard.

"At mealtime, the men sat on split-log benches. Two of their favorite meals were lobscouse and duff. Lobscouse was a combination finely pounded hard tack, bits of salt beef, and potatoes boiled together in water and seasoned with salt and pepper. Duff was considered a luxury in the camps. It was a heavy, dark, and clammy mixture made from flour, water, raisins, and beef fat, which was called slush. After it was boiled for several hours in a canvas bag, it was served with molasses. After every meal, tea 'strong enough to float an axe' was served to aid digestion. The tea was brewed by combining three gallons of water, a pint of tea, and a pint and a half of molasses. It was boiled in a large black pot over the fire and stirred with a stick."

"Cutting timber was done with a simple axe," Jack told them.

"Each man purchased his own cutting edge or bit, as it was known, and then carved his own handle or helve from hickory or hard maple. No self-respecting cutter would purchase a handle. Each handle was custom-made to fit the hands of the cutter."

"How long did it take to cut down a tree?" Tom asks.

"It took a long time. Live oak is so tough that each cutter had to sharpen his axe every thirty minutes," replies Old Jake.

"Once a tree was felled, they had to haul it for shipment. This was done with a team of oxen and a logging cart on big wheels ranging from seven feet to twelve feet in diameter. It took a lot of skill to load a 'stick' onto a cart. The teamster had to find the balance point, tilt the cart backward, and pass a heavy chain under the stick and hook it with a pole. If the cart tipped over backward, the driver could have been crushed by the tongue, the long beam protruding from the axle which allow the oxen to be hitched or the wheels. In fact, we had several serious accidents and one death cutting live oak.

"One of the problems I often overheard Master Miller complain about was the expense to feed the oxen. We had one hundred oxen, and they had to be fed daily. Each ox ate about twenty-six pounds of corn and fourteen pounds of hay.

"Oxen are the best animals for hauling logs out of the woods. Horses are nervous, and mules will panic if their feet get mired in the mud. Oxen can pull longer and harder and are very seldom sick. Sometimes you would see as many as fourteen oxen skid a log down to the landing. You knew that was a heavy piece of live oak."

Old Jake finishes his story, or so it seems. "That's enough for today. It's getting late. But come by tomorrow. I have lots more to tell."

Amos, Amelia, and Tom plead for Old Jake to continue.

"No. I'm old and tired." Old Jake taps his pipe ashes onto the hearth. When Amos, Amelia, and Tom realize it is dark outside, they leave.

"What else can he possibly tell us?" Amelia asks.

"Yeah! How much more do you need to know about cutting trees?" quips Tom.

"I don't think Old Jake only wants to tell us about cutting timber," says Amos. "He has something else on his mind."

The next morning Amos works in the stables, Amelia helps Mammy Esther in the summer kitchen, and Tom tends his father's garden. In the afternoon they meet and immediately run to Old Jake's. Excited, they sit on the floor next to the hearth to hear his tale.

"Right after the American Revolution, when we were a very small nation, several countries in Africa attacked our merchant ships. They were called the Barbary States. For centuries, their Ottoman rulers demanded ransom to trade in their ports from European powers and became very wealthy. These Barbary pirates would high- jack merchant ships and exact a toll. By 1795, our government had paid one-sixth of our national budget in ransom. This had to stop," Jake says.

Amos, Amelia, and Tom sit in disbelief.

"The newly formed Congress of the United States passed the Naval Act of 1794 to build six 74-gun frigates to protect our merchant fleet. Master Miller signed a contract to supply the oak to build one of them. When I was your age, the oak I saw cut was shipped to Boston, Massachusetts, to build the USS *Constitution*." Old Jake tells this part of the story with pride. "It took sixty acres of trees to construct her, all of it cut here."

Far away in Boston, the *Constitution* is built using live oak from Cumberland, Georgia. Joshua Humphrey is the architect who designs her. The oak is so heavy, it requires a special design, one that has not been used before. Humphrey creates a diagonal cross-bracing to prevent the hull from collapsing on its own weight, which allows him to create higher masts. When the *Constitution* is in full sail, an acre of sailcloth pushes her rapidly through the seas. This design allows the ship to outmaneuver and outrun any frigate from any navy in the world. The *Constitution* is so heavy it takes three attempts to launch her. On the first day, she slides twenty-seven feet down the ways. The following day, after some reconstruction, she slides another thirty-one feet before the ways collapsed. A month later, on October 21, 1797, after the ways are totally rebuilt, she slips into Boston harbor. To prevent shipworm, Paul Revere installs copper sheathing on the hull. The *Constitution* is sent immediately to North Africa to defeat the Barbary pirates in the first Barbary War.

On June 18, 1812, war is declared between the United States and Great Britain. British deopredations on the high seas particulary the impressment of American sailors, caused the U.S. to declare war against Britian.The *Constitution* set sail on July 12, 1812, to begin an illustrious career in naval warfare. In her first engagement, she outruns five British ships near Egg Harbor, New Jersey. Using a variety of strategies, the ship's commander, Admiral Issac Hull is able to outrun the British squadron in a fifty-seven-hour chase on the high seas. After replenishing her supplies in Boston, Hull sets sail, without orders, to avoid a British blockade. The HMS *Guerriere* is sighted on August 19. She opens fire on the *Constitution* and thus opens a chapter in history. Her opening salvo does little damage. Hull begins his assault and maneuvers into range. He orders a broadside, which tears down the *Guerriere's* mizzen mast. In extremely close combat, the *Constitution and Guerriere* collide. The shockwaves from the collision topple the foremast of the British ship, and soon the main mast follows. With all her masts destroyed, the *Guerriere* surrenders. A third of her crew is wounded or killed. During the intense exchange, the sailors notice that cannon balls are bouncing off the *Constitution's* hull. One sailor exclaims, "Huzzah! Her sides are made of iron!" and the *Constitution* acquires the nickname "Old Ironsides." For the remainder of the war, the *Constitution* remains undefeated.

This is the first time Amos, Amelia, and Tom hear the history of the live oak on their island. They are fascinated. "What else happened?" they cry in unison to Old Jake.

"Well, believe it or not, this is just the beginning of the story," Old Jake says. "It was the live oak from this island that made the *Constitution* the most-famous naval vessel in the world."

"How do you know all that?" Tom asks.

"I told you once before, I listen to people around me. Before the war was over, many folks on the island would be directly affected by it, including me."

"You too?" they exclaim. "How?"

"I am tired," Old Jake says. He leans back in his chair and closes his eyes. "Come by tomorrow, and I will tell you about my frightful experience with Sir George Cockburn, admiral of the British fleet.

During the War of 1812, the *Constitution* savages British frigates, never losing a battle. With equal ferocity, Sir George Cockburn creates mayhem in Chesapeake Bay. He raids ports and plantations that supported the American war effort. Under orders from his majesty's government, Cockburn impresses American sailors and frees slaves in Virginia and the Carolinas. The freed slaves become British marines. These acts infuriate plantation owners, but they have no way to recover their property.

On August 24, 1814, Cockburn captures and burns Washington City, the nation's capital. Dolly Madison, wife of President James Madison, rescues John Turnbull's famous portrait of George Washington. Shortly afterward, the British forces are defeated during their attack of Baltimore. On a ship in Baltimore harbor, watching the bombs burst in air, Francis Scott Key is inspired to write *The Star-Spangled Banner*.

When Cockburn finally reaches Georgia, he becomes commander of the occupation of Cumberland Island and Saint Mary's, Georgia. For several months, he lives at Dungeness. He orders his crew to cut live oak for the British navy. The war is over, but no one knows it.

Amos, Amelia, and Tom are excited to hear more of Old Jake's story. After their chores, they run to his cabin. Tom raps on the newly whitewashed door. As the door opens, the sun rushes in like a crashing wave and fills the room with light. On the left, against the wall, stands a narrow, low wooden bed. Against the opposite wall is a water bench with basins. In the middle, Old Jake sits on a cane chair. These are his only worldly possessions.

"What else happened?" they ask in unison.

Old Jake takes a bandanna from his pocket and blows his nose. He looks into the brilliant sunlight and squints his eyes.

"Early one morning, I was carrying water from one of the cisterns to the summer kitchen. Out across the field, two field hands were running toward the main house. They had come from the north end. Miss Caty and Master Miller stepped out onto the veranda. They looked agitated.

A British ship had been sighted and was sailing toward the island. I overheard their conversation. 'What's going to happen to us? The plantation?' Master Miller asked."

Caty Greene, an amateur botanist, has filled the acres surrounding Dungeness with gardens and orchards. She builds greenhouses and grows exotic species from all over the world. One of her enterprises, prior to the War of 1812, is to sell citrons from her orchard to the British navy. Citrons prevent scurvy. Perhaps this business relationship stops Cockburn from plundering Dungeness.

"I heard Miss Caty say, 'We have no choice but to invite the commander of that ship into our home.' At the time, no one knew the commander was Sir George Cockburn or about his reign of terror in Virginia and the Carolinas. As his ship sailed into the sound, many of the slaves on the shore saw large numbers of black men on its deck. Anxiety spread like a brush fire among the slaves.

"Master Miller told me to go to the wharf and help the British sailors unload their gear. Out on the deck stepped the commander. He wore a navy-blue jacket with a double row of brass buttons and gold epaulets on his shoulders. A red sash cut diagonally across his jacket, and I saw several medals. In his hand he carried a brass telescope.

"From the deck, Sir George Cockburn's voice boomed like a canon. 'This island of Cumberland and adjacent Saint Mary's town is captured by order of His Majesty's government,' he proclaimed. 'It is now under British jurisdiction.' He pointed his telescope at Dungeness. 'Seize that estate, the estate of the famous American general Nathaniel Greene. It is now my headquarters!'

"And with that order, Cockburn and his staff installed themselves on the top two floors of Dungeness. During the next six months, Cockburn enlisted his crew and the several hundred slaves he'd liberated to cut live oak. The British navy had suffered greatly at the hands of the *Constitution* and other American frigates built from live oak. He was determined to regain sovereignty of the seas. Live oak would restore British supremacy.

"When his ship, the *Rappollo*, was loaded, he prepared to set sail. He ordered his crew to round up as many slaves as possible on the island, free them, and induct them into the British navy as members of the Corps of Colonial Marines.

"I'll never forget that day," Old Jake laments. "On my way to the main house two British marines stopped me. 'Come with us,' they ordered. As we walked toward the ship, I saw about forty field hands getting on board. Cheers rose from the deck. 'You're free! You're free!'

"The cheers pierced through me like a mini ball. I realized I was going to set sail and leave the island forever. I was not free. I had been kidnapped."

"What did you do?" ask the children.

"Nothing, I was herded onto the deck. Many of the field hands were jubilant. I felt suffocated by all the commotion. And soon the sails were unfurled, and the *Rappollo* had set sail for her first destination, Bermuda."

What Sir George did not know when he set sail for Bermuda in January 1815 is that the War of 1812 was over for a month. The *Treaty of Ghent was* signed in December 1814. By illegally cutting the live oak and stealing American property (freeing the slaves), Cockburn had unwittingly committed two offenses with international repercussions. In the centuries before electronic communication, it is weeks at a minimum and very often many months before messages are received. Sir George Cockburn learned about the treaty on his way to Bermuda from newspapers carried by a packet ship. He is not alone; the war continues for many others, most notably Andrew Jackson, soon to become president of the United States, who defeats the British at the Battle of New Orleans after the treaty was signed. The British surrendered on January 8, 1815.

The treaty to end the war is misinterpreted by the British navy. The liberation of American slaves and their recruitment into the Corps of Colonial Marines leads to a two-year exchange of letters between the American and British governments before the terms of the treaty could be resolved. James Monroe, US secretary of state, sends a letter to President James Madison and Mr. Baker, the British chargé de affairs.

> I regret to have to state that the commander of His Britannic Majesty's naval forces in the Chesapeake, and on Cumberland Island, and other islands of the southern coast, have construed the stipulation in the first article of the treaty of peace, lately concluded between the United States and Great Britain, very differently from what is thought to be a just construction of it by this government.

> The issue at stake is the difference between public and private property. Forts and artillery are examples of public property, whereas slaves are private property. In essence what Sir Cockburn did was to steal slaves (personal property) in spite of the fact he thought he had liberated them during war. The war [was] over before he left Cumberland Island. And the treaty stipulates that he return them.

"How did you get back to the island?" Amelia asks.

"I was lucky, I guess," says Old Jake. "For several weeks, I stayed in Bermuda, in limbo. No one knew what to do with us. We were told that we would be sent back to our former owners. I was overjoyed but kept my thoughts to myself. The look of despair and disappointment that washed over the faces of many told me their lives were in peril. I knew what troubles they had been through; they were beaten and their families had been broken up in slave auctions."

Old Jake stands and slowly walks to the door. He looks out across the plantation. He sees cotton fields in bloom, orchards hanging with plump pears, and several schooners at the boat landing. "Maybe I am lucky. I don't ever want to leave this island," he says. "Several weeks later an American schooner arrived, bound for Saint Mary's. The British authorities put me on board." Old Jake has a contented smile.

"A few years after my return we had another visitor—this time a famous American," he says

"Who?"

A warm breeze blows across the island from the south. The pungent smell of tidal wrack mixed with the sweet scent of sea grass wafts to the main house. It is early March 1815. A late winter keeps the island unseasonable cool. And the breeze of natural smells, evocative of things to come, is a well- received augur of spring.

A schooner is spotted. Its bright white sails, like weathered shells, contrast with the blue-green water of the sound. The bell rings in the main house to alert everyone to the ship's imminent arrival. A throng of excited house guests and slaves gather as a welcoming committee and proceed to the dock. The schooner is unexpected. A hushed murmur of voices infects the gathering.

"Who is on board? And what do they want?"

The sails are lowered as the ship approaches the dock. Deck hands secure the lines. A small boarding party emerges from the cabin.

"Where's the old general?" a feeble voice cries. "Where's the old general?"

"It's Harry!" says someone in the crowd. "Light Horse Harry Lee!"

Miss Caty recognizes the voice and ran to the dock. "Light Horse" Harry Lee and General Nathaniel Greene fought together in the American Revolution. Lee is the only soldier under the rank of general to receive a gold medal from the Continental Congress for his actions at the Battle of Paulus Hook in New Jersey. And here is the old man at Dungeness. She and he are old friends. She runs to him and embraces him with tears in her eyes.

"Caty, it's been a long time," he says. "Where's Nat?"

She tells him the general is dead. Lee pauses and then, perhaps remembering their campaigns, looks down. He takes a deep breath. "I thought maybe I might see him one last time," he says sadly. His eyes redden as tears begin to fall.

Three weeks later, "Light Horse" Harry Lee, father of Robert E. Lee, is dead. Before his arrival on Cumberland Island, he has been in the West Indies recuperating from severe wounds suffered while protecting a friend, Alexander Coutee Hanson, editor of a Baltimore newspaper, *The Federal Republican*. Because the editor is opposed to the War of 1812, one day, a mob breaks into the newspaper office and severely beat Hanson and Lee.

On March 25, 1818, Light Horse Harry Lee dies at Dungeness, the home of his friends Caty and General Nathaniel Greene. Out of respect for his wartime and government service to his country, the largest-ever US Navy flotilla anchors off Saint Mary's and fires a twenty-one gun salute.

Amos, Amelia, and Tom are amazed to hear the history of their island. It takes Tom stubbing his toe on an old template for them to discover they live in a very important place.

"Boy, I am sure happy Old Jake is still alive," Tom says.

"He must have a heap of stories to tell us," Amelia adds.

"Yeah, I'm sure he does," Amos agrees.

7

Blockade Runner

"I am going up to Savannah for a few days to meet with the trustees of the Georgia Railroad Company," Mr. Robert announces to Amos and Amelia. "They are trying to build a new line from the port of Savannah to the middle part of the state to move cotton."

Robert Stafford owns one hundred slaves and is willing to lease many of them out to help build rail lines for the new railroad. In return, he accept stocks in the newly formed company, instead of cash.

"The trustees and I need to discuss the terms of the contract," Mr. Robert says as he walks toward the dock and the small sloop *Amelia* that awaits him. The twins plead to go. He reminds them they have chores to do. Also, Mammy Esther needs their help while he is away.

The morning is clear, and the sun rises slowly over the island. A gentle breeze blows off Saint Andrew's Sound. The water is dead calm. Mr. Robert surmises the voyage to Savannah will take the better part of the day. He expects to dock by early evening. The crew untie the lines and raise *Amelia's* sail.

"Good-bye!" Amos and Amelia stand on the dock and wave to Mr. Robert.

The mainsail is swept by the breeze and propels her into the channel. "Due north, we're Savannah bound," Mr. Robert tells the crew. The *Amelia* sails past the Union blockade. Mr. Robert marvels at the many ships they sail past—single-paddle wheelers, double-paddle wheelers, newly built iron-clad ships with screws, and several older wooden-hulled ships still using great sheets of sail. All of the ships are well armed; some have mortars, but most have a variety of deck guns. To a small sloop, these ships are menacing, with their blue-black guns that in a second can be trained and fired at will.

The *Amelia* sails through the blockade without challenge, then out of the sound and on its journey through the Intracoastal Waterway, passing the ports of Darien and Brunswick. Mr. Robert thinks about his upcoming meeting with the railroad trustees but also about the dangers faced by Confederate blockade runners as they try to outrun these large Union gunboats.

The sun rises steadily like the mercury in a thermometer throughout the morning warming the crew on the *Amelia*. The air over the mainland heats and rises. The convection currents draw moisture off the ocean, which creates a strong sea breeze. Usually by noon, the water-saturated air is carried into the cold upper strata, and clouds form. In the afternoon, these "popcorn" clouds are full of energy and produce squalls and violent thunderstorms.

"Cleo," Mr. Robert warns his skipper. "You keep your eyes on those clouds. I have been in a couple of bad blows. If they start to move in this direction when the wind backs around, you head straight for the nearest port."

"Oh, I know," says Cleo. "I remember three years ago when the weather was very much like it is today. Jon went over to Saint Mary's and got caught in the leading edge of a squall line in the sound, and his boat sank. It came up so fast he didn't have time to reef the sail."

The crew watch the cloud formations and check the wind as the *Amelia* sails toward Savannah. They pass the islands of Jekyll and Saint Simon's and sail all the way to Wassau Sound. Late in the afternoon, Mr. Robert orders the *Amelia* to sail into the sound. He tells the crew to prepare for the final twelve miles up the Savannah River. Union ships are everywhere. Great clouds of black smoke stream across the sound from the single- and double-stacked gunboats that prevent Confederate ships from entering or exiting Savannah. On the leeward side stands Fort Pulaski, with its imposing walls of brick and cannons aimed toward the sea. The Georgia state flag flutters in the breeze. Several months earlier, Governor Brown orders the Georgia militia to capture the fort from the only two Union soldiers stationed there. It is a blow to the Union but essential to the survival of the Confederacy. Fort Pulaski protects the city of Savannah, a trading port and rail hub. If Savannah is captured, the Confederacy will not survive.

Mr. Robert turns to Cleo and says, "Boy, there's a lot of military activity here. Just look at all those ships."

"Yes, sir," Cleo replies. "Those Yankees are trying to strangle us, keep us from getting food and supplies. We are in for some hard times."

"Yes, Cleo, but even in hard times some people make money," Mr. Robert says.

The *Amelia* tacks through the Union blockade and into the mouth of the Savannah River. Soon Mr. Robert sees Old Fort Jackson, a structure from the War of 1812 that now is used for the Confederate defense of Savannah, which is heavily fortified. The palisades of Savannah rise before him. A bluff that rises up from the river and lowland swamps dominate the area; it is a perfect site for a city. The long docks and wharfs creep out into the river to welcome the incoming traffic from England, Nassau, Havana, and Bermuda. Small sloops, similar to Mr. Robert's, brigs, four-masters, and newly built steamers with long black smoke stacks that reach toward the sky are all docked along the waterfront. Stevedores of every hue and shape load and unload cargo, destined to or coming from all ports in the world.

Directly across the river is Hutchinson Island. It is filled with docks, boat houses, and warehouses. Before the war, both sides of the river teemed with maritime activity. Even now, despite the Union blockade, the port still functions. Blockade runners continue to elude the Yankees. A thin trickle of cargo keeps the Confederacy alive and, more important, offers hope.

"Pull aside here," Mr. Robert orders Cleo. "I want to take a look at that ship over there."

A brand new ship with the name *Bermuda* painted across the stern attracts Mr. Robert's attention. It is an iron-hulled screw-driven merchantman with a large cargo capacity. As the *Amelia* slowly sails past, Mr. Robert notices a large amount of cargo being unloaded.

"I want to meet that captain," Mr. Robert says to Cleo. "See how close we can dock to her."

"Yes, sir!" Cleo skillfully maneuvers the *Amelia* into a slip beside the new merchantman.

Mr. Robert jumps from the *Amelia* on to the dock and in a few minutes is standing alongside the *Bermuda*. Several strong black men unload large boxes of cargo with a block and tackle. Mr. Robert notices many of the boxes are stamped "England" on the side. The men use the block and tackle to haul the cargo from the ship's hold and set it on the dock.

"Ahoy, mates!" Mr. Robert yells. "Where is your captain?"

In a few minutes, a tall, bronze-skinned man with a black mustache and wavy black hair appears on the deck. "Sir, I'm Eugene L. Tessier. How can I help you?"

"I couldn't help notice the large amount of cargo you are unloading," Mr. Robert replies. "Did you have any trouble with the Union gunboats out in Wassau Sound?"

"Nah," Tessier says with pride. "This boat is very fast and easily slips past them. A few nights ago when the fog was heavy, I made my run. No one spotted us."

"What type of cargo do you carry?" Mr. Robert asks.

"We have shoes, blankets, dry goods, and medicines not to mention the military supplies. I have eighteen field pieces, four heavy seacoast guns, about 6,500 Enfield rifles and twenty thousand cartridges—all for sale to the highest bidder."

Like a flock of vultures, several officials and private businessmen descend upon the *Bermuda*. General Lawton of Savannah seizes three thousand Enfield rifles. "This will supply several Georgia regiments," he boasts.

The remaining small arms and field pieces are sent to the Confederate States Army in Virginia. Amid complaints of high prices, the balance of the cargo is sold to merchants and Confederate officials.

Mr. Robert looks at the unloaded cargo and is impressed. "When are you sailing again?" he asks.

"Perhaps, in a few days," Tessier says. "We need to load about two thousand bales of cotton. I'll try to get it into Nassau and sell it there. Once I get past the Yankees out in the sound, it is clear sailing."

Tessier doesn't yet know he will be delayed. It isn't until late October that he will set sail—not for Nassau, but for England to sell the cotton. When the vessel arrives in mid-November, it will discharge the cargo, which will be sold on the struggling English cotton market for a huge profit.

Mr. Robert looks Tessier straight in the eye and says. "I've got four hundred bales of cotton down on Cumberland Island I want to sell."

"That's not for me," Tessier says. "The water there is too shallow for this boat. You will need a center-board or flat-bottom boat. I know just the skipper who can do it for you. His name is Jesse Buckland. He has nerves of steel and isn't afraid to take a risk. He doesn't want the Yankees to win this war and, of course, he doesn't mind making a profit."

"Where can I find this skipper?" Mr. Robert asks.

"He is usually at the *Eye of the Needle*, a tavern on the corner of River Street and Factor's Walk. Not a hard place to find," Tessier tells him.

Mr. Robert thanks him for his help and walks over to the *Amelia*. "Cleo, stand fast," he says. "I'll be back shortly."

He has several things to do, including finding Jesse Buckland, who might help him sell his cotton before it rots. He steps off the dock onto the flag-paved street and toward one of the many three-story brick cotton warehouses at Factor's Walk. When Savannah was first settled, the flags and cobblestone in the streets along the waterfront were made from ballast collected from incoming English ships.

Mr. Robert heads straight for the Eye of the Needle, opens the heavy black-green door, and walks into a large, smoke-filled room. Sawdust is sprinkled on the heavy heart pine planks. The air smells of resin and sour ale. Customers talk, smoke, and play a variety of board games. Jesse Buckland spends much of his time at the tavern when he's not running cotton out of South Georgia past the Union blockade.

Mr. Robert asks the barkeep, "Where can I find Jesse Buckland?"

"Who wants to know?" calls a voice from the back of the room.

"Tell him Robert Stafford of Cumberland Island wants to speak with him," responds Mr. Robert. "I want to employ him."

"Over here, Mr. Stafford," Jesse calls from the back. "I know your plantation well. What can I do for a man of your stature?"

"Let's talk about this quietly, perhaps outside where no one will hear." Mr. Robert speaks softly.

The two men walk outside and into the shadows. Night has fallen, and the lamps are lit along the waterfront. Stars fill the night sky. The Savannah River runs black and strong out to the sea.

"I have four hundred bales of cotton I need to sell," Mr. Robert says.

"They should bring a hefty profit," Jesse says.

"Can you get them to market for me?" Mr. Robert asks.

"No problem, but the time and tide needs to be just right. I know your island well. I grew up at Saint Mary's and know the sandbars and the tides like the back of my hand. The union fleet has to stay out in the main channel. I can slip in close to your dock, load the cotton, skirt the island, and make a break for the open sea by Fort Clinch."

"When is the best time?" Mr. Robert asks.

"The best time is during fog. No one can see, and sound is muffled," Jesse replies.

"Okay. Then during the next fog, we will load cotton." Mr. Robert negotiates a contract with Buckland, the skipper of the blockade runner *Mary Elizabeth*, and waits for the right time.

Eventually, fog descends over the island. It cloaks the loblolly pine and live oak like a great overcoat. It creeps into the slave quarters and sucks the dryness from the rooms. It creates a haze across the meadow and obscures the herds of grazing deer. It encloses the island like a tabby wall. No one in; no one out. Fog filters into the saw palm and undergrowth of the maritime forest; like splinters of sunlight, it pierces the canopy. It reaches down to touch the leaves, turned brown from tannin. It smothers the marsh.

This is the moment Mr. Robert is waiting for. His four hundred bales of cotton lie waiting for the fog and Jesse Buckland. They need to be sold. Though the Union boats patrol the sound from Fernandina to Saint Mary's to the Satilla River, Buckland with his small swift blockade runner can easily elude them in fog like this. Once out of the sound, he can set course for Bermuda, Nassau, or Havana. If the venture is successful, Mr. Robert will realize an immense profit. The cotton will be sold to English buyers and the revenue used to purchase much-needed supplies, like ammunition, shoes, clothing, and medical supplies, for the Confederate war effort. The South needs to sell cotton, and Mr. Robert has plenty to sell.

Amos and Amelia finish their chores in the kitchen. They notice Mr. Robert pacing the heart-pine floors, unaware of their presence. He seems lost in thought. Fog wraps Planter's House like an envelope. No one can see farther than a few yards. The tabby wall—usually clear and formidable—is absorbed into the fog. Startled, Mr. Robert sees the twins standing by the mahogany secretary, which houses his records, accounts, and correspondence. A black leather bound account book is open, and ink and quill lie nearby. The twins realize that he has been working on his accounts. Due to the heat of the dayMr. Robert usually works on his accounts in the coolof the evening. But why tonight?

"Amelia! You and Amos, come here." He summons them. "Run over to Mr. James, and tell him tonight's the night. He'll know what I mean."

Amos and Amelia leave Planter's House and push into the fog. "Amos, you stay close," says Amelia. "I don't want to get lost."

The moisture presses against their faces. They feel like dish rags not yet wrung out. Hand in hand, they walk down the carriage drive, through the main gate, and onto the road. They turn right and walk to the end of the tabby wall.

"Can you see Mr. James's house?" Amelia asks.

Amos peers through the fog. The moisture is so dense that small droplets of water drip from the trees. "It's that one over there," he says to Amelia. They walk up to the house, and Amos knocks on the slat door.

"Who's out there?" a voice rumbles from inside.

"Amos! Mr. Robert says tonight's the night."

Mr. James appears in the light of the open door. Tall, black, and muscular, he throws on a roughly woven cotton shirt and quietly closes the door. "Let's go!"

He lets out the long, low call of a mourning dove. The twins listen. From the fog bank comes a reply and then another. "Good," says Mr. James. "We've got all the help we'll need."

Soon Amelia and Amos hear the snort of an ox and the creaking rumble of a wagon. Several field hands sit quietly in the back. Amos, Amelia, and Mr. James walk behind the wagon.

"You get up to the Little field tract," Mr. James softly tells the wagon driver. "That's where Mr. Robert's cotton is stored."

The air presses against them. Droplets of sweat trickle down Amos's arms. Amelia's shirt is soaked, and she feels uncomfortable. A muffled crack erupts from the woods.

"What's that?" Amelia asks.

"Just another critter," Amos replies.

The team slowly moves past Planter's House and heads for the north end of the island. An eerie glow emanates from the study window. Like apparitions, shadows pace back and forth.

"Not far to go." Mr. James speaks in a hushed voice.

The team of oxen turns off the main road as if they've been programmed to do so and plods toward a large open shed. Bales of cotton, freshly ginned, wait to be sold.

The *Mary Elizabeth*, a two-mast schooner, is docked, her sails reefed. Amos and Amelia peer at the ship. All they can see is the deck, cabin, and the lower spars. The fog and darkness obscure the masts. It looks as if the tops of the masts have evaporated into the heavy mist. The hatches are open and ready to load the bales. Jesse tells Mr. James to load as many bales as possible in the hold. The rest will be secured on the deck with strong cord made from Manila hemp.

Throughout the night, under Mr. James's supervision, four hundred bales are transported from the shed and loaded on the *Mary Elizabeth*. Twenty slaves work all night in absolute silence. They cannot be detected loading contraband. The Union gunboats are anchored only three hundred yards away.

The sky lightens as dawn approaches, but the fog holds. Jesse waves his arms, and the lines are released. Amos and Amelia watch intently as the schooner drifts into the fog and disappears completely. She is on her way to Nassau.

It is the third voyage for the *Mary Elizabeth* during this first year of the Civil War. Jessie Buckland, a seasoned skipper, knows these waters well. He is both a patriot and a profiteer. He does not want the Union to destroy his way of life, whose foundation lies in slavery, although he does not own slaves. Also, as an entrepreneur, he wants to make as much money as he can.

Blockade running is a risky enterprise; nearly a fourth of runners are captured or run aground and their cargos either confiscated or destroyed. Tropical storms, squall lines, and sand bars are problems. But the major threats are Union gunboats whose job is to destroy the blockade runners on whom the lifeline of the Confederacy depends.

From Planter's Wharf, the *Mary Elizabeth* hugs the shoreline. She is called a center-board boat and is designed for just such voyages. The bays and estuaries along the South Georgia coast and the outflow of the major rivers create bars of shallow water. Vessels with deeper draughts cannot enter those areas. The *Mary Elizabeth* is built in a particular way to ensure her seaworthiness. Her dimensions and proportions are strictly observed and make her stable and seaworthy; otherwise she would be too dangerous to sail. A proportion of 1:6 in the rise from the floor, from keel to bilge, is complemented by the breadth of the beam, which is no less than 3.5 times the depth of the hold. The keel, which must be of great breadth and strength, extends only a few inches below the planking of the bottom. A slot is cut in the center of the keel to receive the center board, which can be raised up and down. The center board helps hold up the vessel and prevents it from drifting leeward.

The *Mary Elizabeth* has an advantage as a blockade runner. Because the center board can be raised and lowered, she can navigate shoals and bars where a deep vessel could not. She is constructed perfectly for her run from Cumberland Island to Nassau.

Amos and Amelia leave the dock and walk to Planter's House. The *Mary Elizabeth*, wrapped in fog like a great patterned quilt, sails toward the entrance of Cumberland Sound. The eight-man crew includes

Skipper Jesse Buckland, the mate, cook, cabin boy, and four seamen. They skillfully maneuvered the schooner between the shoreline and the channel where the ships of the Union blockade stand watch. Several times the crew raise the center board as they slide over sand bars. Soon they are on the western shore of the island, and safe. The fog remains dense.

Jesse turns to his mate, Johnny, an old Scotsman, and says "We need to sail out under low canvas. The fog and darkness will make it impossible to be seen by Union gunboats. Once we get past them, raise the sails and make a break for it."

"Aye, aye, captain!" Johnny replies. In his Scottish brogue, he orders the crew. "Double reef the mainsail and foresail, and secure the lines for a heavy strain."

There is little wind, and the water is smooth as silk.

What Jesse, Johnny, and the crew do not anticipate is the fog is lifting on the southern and eastern sides of the island. Jessie is surprised to see the sky lighten as he sails the *Mary Elizabeth* toward the entrance to the sound. A splinter of sunlight, like a shower of arrows, pierces through the fog and reflects off the sea. He sees the green fronds of the cabbage palm that grows all over the North Florida coast and the Union flag flying over Fort Clinch.

"Stand to," Jessie orders the crew.

Just then, the wind shifts, and within minutes the ominous outlines of several gunboats are visible. Jesse quietly calls out, "Can you see the black smoke on the horizon, Johnny? That's from that gunboat with the single smokestack. Can you see the Yankee flag fluttering off her stern?"

Johnny says, "Skipper, we can see them. I wonder if they can see us."

The *Mary Elizabeth* has one more advantage: at least for a few more minutes, the sun will shine directly out of the East and into the eyes of the Union sailors on watch. The schooner is painted white; with her sails reefed, she is difficult to see. All she needs is a few minutes; then Jesse orders the sails to be raised. "Make a break," he orders.

The crew, alert, quickly raises both the mainsail and foresail. The wind catches both canvasses, and the crew feels the immediate acceleration as she cuts through the water.

Caleb, the cabin boy, is first to notice one of the Union gunboats coming about. He yells to the captain. "The guns are pointed toward us."

Jesse orders Johnny to tack into the wind. The *Mary Elizabeth* circumscribes an arc as she heads directly into the oncoming waves.

Caleb calls out, "I see a flash from one of the cannons."

Around the same time, everyone hears the shot, and a large splash of water like a geyser explodes just off the stern.

"Wow!,that was to close.They have us in their range." Jesse yells to the crew. "Keep on tacking until we get out of their range."

Jessie sees two more gunboats begin to turn. "There trying to get to us!" he yells to the crew. "Use the wind blowing in from the southeast," he commands.

The gunboats, which have been broadside a few minutes earlier, lose their advantage. All the gunners see now is the stern of the *Mary Elizabeth.* Johnny successfully tacks, and now she is running on a brisk wind, out toward the open waters of the Atlantic Ocean.

Frustrated, the Union gunners fire a few more shots in desperation. They fall far from their mark. Now cannons from Fort Clinch are firing on the *Mary Elizabeth.* The fog hasn't totally lifted and still obscures the view from the batteries. Luck has followed the *Mary Elizabeth* thus far on her fourth mission. *Will it continue,* Jesse wonders?

Johnny corrects course and runs parallel to the Florida coast; his destination is Nassau and huge profits.

"We've got a three-day voyage ahead of us if nothing happens," Jesse tells the crew.

Out of immediate danger, the crew settles in for the trip to Nassau. A pod of dolphins race the *Mary Elizabeth* and playfully cross the bow. Caleb watches in fascination. Tall green coconut trees reach toward the sky. Slow-moving spilling breakers crash over the hidden sand bars onto the pure white sand beaches as the *Mary Elizabeth* descends the Florida coast. The sky explodes blue as iced diamonds. The two sails go slack. A great calm descends over the *Mary Elizabeth* as the wind drops.

Jesse turns to Johnny. "I don't like the feel of the air. The energy is being sucked out. We are in for a blow."

Jesse is an able skipper. He watches and feels the air around him.

Like the ancient mariners, he relies upon his instincts to forecast the weather. He knows the ocean by the rhythm of the currents beneath him. He constantly watches the sky for signs of change. High wispy clouds called mare's tails usually foretell storms. A ring around the moon predicts rain in the near future. Rising or falling smoke indicates barometric pressure.

The hurricane season is over. Starting in June and continuing through September, hurricanes plague merchantmen in the Straits of Florida and along the Atlantic seaboard. Cumberland Island has been spared many a hurricane because of its location. However, this is not true of areas to the east or south. Freak tropical storms are always a hazard.

Without wind, a sailing ship is subject to the whim of currents. Without wind, the *Mary Elizabeth* drifts to the south, gently pushed by the current.

"This reminds me of the doldrums," Jesse says to Johnny. "The air is still as a stake. If this keeps up, we might be dead in the water for days."

"We have enough fresh water and food for several more days," Johnny replies.

"Don't worry, this won't last long. We are in for a big blow and soon," Jesse says.

Late in the afternoon, the sky becomes very dark. Off to the southeast, the crew observes a line of thunder heads develop. An ominous breeze kicks up. The wind increases in velocity. The sails that earlier hung from the spars listlessly now snap in the wind.

"Haul those sails before they get ripped off," orders Jesse.

The crew immediately reefs the sails. Whitecaps whipped by the wind slap against the hull. Water crashes over the bow into the boat. The *Mary Elizabeth* lurches into the oncoming waves and slides down into the trough. Green and white bubbly foam skims the boat. The sky darkens and sheets of rain pelt the *Mary Elizabeth*.

"Make sure the lines are secure on the bales of cotton," Jesse hollers over the roar of the wind.

The storm develops so fast, the crew doesn't have time to put on their foul weather gear. Soaked by the rain and the water crashing over the bow, they secure the bales of cotton. Great rumbles of thunder interrupt the howling wind. The sky bursts into cold white as lighting dances from cloud to cloud and from cloud to the sea.

"Get below!" Jessie yells. "You'll be washed overboard!"

Suddenly, a tremendous whistling sound roars through the rigging. The wind snaps the top of the main mast, which dangles helplessly. The wind pushes the waves higher and higher. Wave after wave pounds the hull of the disabled schooner. Four hundred pound bales of cotton strain the lines until at last, one snaps. And, in quick succession, like dominos, bales of cotton slide across the deck and tumble into the raging sea.

As quickly as the storm blows up, it dissipates. The wind dies down, the waves subside, and the sky lightens in the west. Jesse and the crew emerge from the hold and survey the damage.

"We can at least limp into Nassau," Jesse reports. "Johnny, let's get that top mast down and repaired. The cotton that was on the deck is lost, and the cotton below is sitting in sea water. Man the pumps," he orders. "We've got to save what's left."

A day later, the *Mary Elizabeth*, under half sail, drifts into the port of Nassau and delivers a portion of Mr. Robert's cotton. The crew is lucky. Twenty-five percent of blockade runners are either captured or sink at sea.

8

Jonkonnu

Christmas takes on a special poignancy in time of war. In the South, many children suffer deprivation during the holiday season. Their parents tell them that Santa Claus is a Yankee and cannot get through Southern picket lines. A Virginia soldier complains that when he visits his grandmother on Christmas Day, he finds Yankee soldiers snatching up stock and forage for their horses. They rip her shed doors off their hinges during their greedy search for provisions. One of the troopers grabs his grandmother by the collar demanding money. On Christmas Day 1864, Moscow Carter, a Virginian farmer, laments because he has to borrow a yoke of oxen and remove seventeen dead horses from his yard. The Union and Confederates fought a battle the previous day on his farm

General William T. Sherman sends a soon-to-be famous Christmas gift to President Lincoln: "I beg to present to you as a Christmas gift, the city of Savannah, with 100 and 50 guns and plenty of ammunition, also about 25,000 bales of cotton," writes the Union general. Yet there are acts of generosity as well. Sherman's troops play Santa Claus to impoverished Southern children by attaching tree branch antlers to their horses and mules as they deliver food to starving families. On Cumberland Island, isolated from the ravages of war, Christmas is still celebrated as it always has been, despite the deprivations that affect the rest of the South.

A clear sky ushers in the morning. A bracing wind blows from the northwest. It sweeps the dried leaves from the ground and lifts them into the air. Wind eddies swirl them into tight knots, like predator birds circling their prey. The solstice is due within days. The cold snap and bitter wind certainly make everyone feel that winter has descended upon the island.

At Planter's House, activity and expectations run high. In just a few short days, Christmas will be here, and then two days later, they will celebrate Jonkonnu. Amos and Amelia pulse with excitement. There is much to do, and so much fun to look forward to. But first, Mr. Robert's house needs to be decorated.

Amos and Amelia usually work in the kitchen and dining room, but for the next week they will do whatever Old James, Mr. Robert's butler, tells them to do.

"Amos and Amelia," Old James commands. "Go out in the maritime forest and get plenty of holly for decorations. We need to cover the mantles over the fireplaces and have enough for the dining room table and sideboards. And cut some mistletoe as well."

Amos and Amelia race past the Duncan Phyfe mahogany dining table they have just oiled; it gleams in the morning sun. Silver, flatware, and serving utensils of all kinds are stacked on the sideboard, waiting to be polished. Linen napkins are folded and wait to be set in someone's lap. The recently polished heart-pine floors are covered by an Abbuson floral-patterned wool rug, imported from France, that Mr. Robert purchased in Savannah.

The twins bound out the front door and jump off the porch. Amos calls to Amelia, "Come on, let's get bunches of holly!"

They sprint down the lane and across the open field and head straight for the forest. A recent frost flattened the rattlebush and shepherd's needle. The fields lie dry and dormant.

"Boy, it's chilly this morning" Amelia says.

"Run fast, and you'll be warm," Amos says.

A great crash erupts as soon as they enter the forest. Three deer bound over a dead log and into the underbrush. The trees stand tall as ancient giants. The children feel dwarfed by their presence. Spanish moss hangs in great silver strands from the live oaks, and resurrection fern creeps along the lower branches. Sparkleberry, devil's walking stick, and coralroot cover the understory. Amelia picks the hairy basal leaves of elephant's foot.

"Amos," she says. "These purple flowers will look good next to the holly berries. Look there's a holly tree. The leaves are prickly, so watch out."

"Wow! The berries are bright red," says Amos. "They'll be excellent decorations."

A year earlier, Old James selects his six best axe hands to go into the swamps and find the largest, knottiest cypress tree on the island. "Men, you go into the woods just north of Mr. Robert's shed," he says. "I was over here this week, and there are some mighty tall trees. You need to cut the Yule log for next Christmas and Jonkonnu."

The men cut the largest, knottiest tree they can find. When it comes crashing to the ground, they ceremoniously sing the "Coonah" song:

> Christmas comes but once a year
> Ho rang du rango
> Let everybody have a share
> Ho rang du rango.

After they fell the tree, it is measured to fit into Mr. Robert's fireplace and then sunk in one of the small estuaries so that it will become water-logged.

Amos and Amelia hope that the men found the biggest and wettest log so that it will burn forever. As long as the log burns, the celebrations continue. Today, Old James has instructed several men to raise the log from the canal, dry it off, drag it to the main house, and place it in the fireplace. On Christmas, it will burn brightly to begin the holidays.

Amos and Amelia return with the holly and immediately begin to wash and polish the silver.

"How much more do we have to polish?" groans Amos.

"A lot more," replies Amelia. "Mr. Robert has invited many guests, including some Union officers from the blockade, for the holidays. And after we finish the silver, we have to fold all the linens and place them on the table."

Several weeks before the holidays, Old James organizes a food brigade. Much has to be hunted, gathered, picked, slaughtered, and dried to accommodate all the invited guests. Old James sends slaves into the maritime forest to hunt small island deer. The venison makes a succulent roast, turned on spits over burning white coals. Heaps of oysters gathered from the marshes steam in great fire pits until their shells open naturally; they are everyone's favorite. Hogs and cattle are slaughtered. Fowl of every description—geese, ducks, and chickens—are strangled and plucked and make their way to the table roasted, grilled, or fried. The children pick pecans, walnuts, butternuts, and acorns for stuffing and cookies. Vegetables from the larder are washed, peeled, sliced, and chopped.

House slaves carry sheets, pillow cases, and blankets upstairs to prepare extra beds for the guests. The house is a whirlwind of ordered activity. Old James has prepared for the Christmas season many times and knows exactly who will perform which chores, based on age and ability. Everyone on the plantation comes under his watchful eyes.

Finally, Christmas Day arrives. The guests who arrive by boat from Saint Mary's complain about the bracing wind off the water.

"Boy, that wind bit like a rattlesnake," says Darcy Shetland, the banker from Saint Mary's.

"I'll say! I've never been so cold crossing the sound as I was today," says his wife.

Lieutenant Townsend, one of several officers Mr. Robert has invited from the Yankee detachment on the island, extends his hand in greeting to his host. "That's a mighty fierce wind blowing down the sound," he says. "My driver had to remove several large limbs from the road."

The officers who accompany him, dressed in formal attire, wish Mr. Robert a Merry Christmas. Mr. Robert is well known for his generosity at Christmas, and his guests look forward to spending the holiday with him. Throughout the day, people bearing gifts continue to arrive. Many of Mr. Robert's friends from the Camden Hunting Club bring their children, who look forward to the Christmas Eve festivities.

Old James's wife, Esther, affectionately called Mammy by everyone, is responsible for hanging the stockings. The children are wide-eyed as they see their stockings hung over the fireplace or on the knobs of the two sideboards. Mammy hangs her stocking last, over the back of a chair directly in front of the fireplace. A few days after Christmas is over for Mr. Robert and his white friends, Jonkonnu will begin.

Late in the afternoon, the wind that has blustered all day dies down. The largest moon of the season rises in the east over the Atlantic Ocean. The field slaves return to their quarters, excited to talk about the silver moon as large as the sky itself. In the maritime forest, the moon illuminates the strands of Spanish moss that hang from the gnarled limbs of the live oak trees. Shadows leap like court jesters with maniacal smiles, causing the slaves to tremble with fear. They are superstitious. At night, they believe that haints that live in the trees will cause not only mischief but death as well. Safely at home, they send out the word that tonight all of the whites on the island will be at Planter's House celebrating Christmas. In the light of the full moon, slaves gather and light torches. In military fashion, four abreast the slaves fall into line. They march to the cadence of a deerskin drum. The drummer strikes the drum head with a hand-carved, well-oiled piece of white ash. Slaves who cut timber on the north end, slaves who work the cotton fields, and slaves who ferry boats on the sound all join the procession. A primal chant a thousand years old fills the maritime forest with sounds of a distant world. Light from flickering torches reflects off the faces of a hundred or more slaves and illuminates the path to Planter's House. The long procession slowly gathers momentum and marches toward the lights shining through the windows.

The great Yule log is set ablaze with kindling placed earlier in the day. As the flames lick at the sides of the log, the guests burst in to song. "It Came upon a Midnight Clear," "See Amid the Winter's Snow" and "We Three Kings of Orient Are" are sung with much enthusiasm. Planter's House does not have a traditional Christmas tree, because German immigrants—who will introduce that tradition to the United States—have not yet reached this part of the South. Santa Claus however, is awaited with great anticipation. The children plead with Mr. Robert to read Clement Moore's *The Night before Christmas*, which he graciously does.

His voice finds expression when he reads "when out on the lawn there arose such a clatter, I sprang from my bed to see what the matter was." Wide-eyed and in awe, the youngest children listen with intent. The children follow every modulation in his voice and movement of his hands as though mesmerized. When Mr. Robert reads "when, to my wondering eyes should appear, But a miniature sleigh, and eight tiny reindeer," he looks out the window and pauses. The children immediately run to the window to see what is there. When he reads the final verse, "Happy Christmas to all, and to all a good night," the children are sent to bed "while visions of sugar-plums dance in their heads."

"Bravo, Mr. Robert!" echoes a chorus of voices from the adults.

"Please have another glass of the Muscatine wine," offers Mr. Robert. "Oh, and by the way, you might like some of Mammy's eggnog. No one makes it better than she does."

Mammy spends the better part of the early evening cracking eggs into a large bowl; she adds great amounts of sugar and beats the ingredients into a frothy creamy mixture. She then adds generous amounts of liquor. When this is complete, she pours the mixture into a large, elaborately tooled, silver cistern made by Rundell and Bridge, a goldsmith firm in England. The oval cistern, chased with bands of fluting and overlapping stiff foliage, sits on three legs. It has two lion's head, double-scroll ring handles. Mammy says it is so large, you can take a bath in it. Mr. Robert imported it from England many years before and set it on the rosewood sideboard.

During a lull in the festivities, Lieutenant Townsend approaches Mr. Robert with a compliment. "This is the best wine I have ever tasted," he says.

"Thank you, sir. These grapes have grown on the island as long as I can remember. The slaves pick the fruit at the end of the summer and ferment it in the big casks you see outside. It's not quite as good as wine or sherry from France, but with the war and all, we can be thankful the grapes grow here."

A drumbeat echoes through the front door. Startled, the guests turn their heads to the sound. Through the windows, they see a procession of slaves carrying torches. All of Mr. Robert's slaves are marching toward Planter's House. Darcy Shetland's eyes get large as the moon, and he grabs Mr. Robert by the arm.

"Oh, Lord, look at all those Negras. They can kill us all!" he exclaims in terror. "Get a gun. You got to protect us. You've heard about the slave revolts in Virginia and on the islands."

Submerged in the subconscious of every slave owner is the fear that a slave rebellion could erupt at any moment. Like the unpredictability of a hurricane, the tumult of an uprising would ravage Mr. Robert's plantation and perhaps end the lives of his family.

Planters are keenly aware of the Haitian Revolution, which lasted for thirteen years. Between 1791 and 1804, the year Haiti declares independence, the country is embroiled in a slave revolt. Britain dispatches an armada of 218 ships to the Caribbean, and British troops unsuccessfully fight the insurgents for five years before they withdraw. Napoleon sends the largest force that ever sails from France, but the French lose more than fifty thousand soldiers and eighteen generals due to the revolt and disease. Napoleon's force in the Americas is so depleted, he can no longer protect French territory in North America and is forced to sell it to President Thomas Jefferson. The Louisiana Purchase adds thousands of acres to a rapidly expanding United States. The Haitian Revolution greatly inspires people in slavery throughout America.

In 1831, a slave named Nat Turner has a series of religious visions that convince him he is an instrument of God. When the final vision appears, an atmospheric condition in which the sun turns bluish-green, he and six slaves go on a killing spree. Fifty-five white people are killed before he is arrested and hanged. By the time the rebellion is over, Virginia has executed fifty-five of Turner's followers. In addition, in the wake of the hysteria, whites murder more than two hundred black people, many of whom have nothing to do with the insurrection.

"Calm down, Darcy," Mr. Robert says. They are just coming to visit. Every Christmas they march like that and wish us a Merry Christmas."

The house is soon surrounded by chanting slaves. Shadows dance in the flicker of their torches. Then, all of a sudden, the drums stop, and silence reigns.

"A toast for Mr. Robert" a voice calls. "Merry Christmas to you and your family!"

Mr. Robert opens the door and welcomes the slaves onto the veranda. "Mammy, serve our guests a glass of eggnog." As they pass, he shakes each of their hands and bids them a Merry Christmas too.

The next morning, Christmas Day, the slaves return and assemble on the front veranda. Several hampers are filled with gifts. Mr. Robert gives money to his slaves—fifty cents in silver to the men and a quarter to the women. Several of the guests also distribute gifts to the slaves. Colored cloth, madras handkerchiefs, comforters, gloves, balls, tops, knives, and pipes are received by all. The married women march straight to the larder or storehouse to "draw Christmas," which means getting an extra allotment of meat, molasses, rice, coffee, and dried fruit to make their holiday feasts.

At precisely three o'clock in the afternoon, Old James rings the bell. He summons the guests to Christmas dinner. The men and women arrive from two different rooms. In the library, several men with glasses of brandy are conducting a spirited conversation about the progress of the war. They find their way to the table, while their wives gracefully move from the parlor to join them. An argument begins between Darcy Shetland and Albert Lynch.

"Governor Brown is destroying our chances of wining this war by opposing the draft President Davis wants," Darcy says.

"Davis was stupid to secede from the Union," Albert Lynch responds in a loud voice. "This war is breaking our backs. I can't sell cotton because of the blockade. What good is a war if it means financial ruin? I have spent all my life building a business, and to lose it because of a few hotheads in Virginia … Is this war about patriotism or poverty?

Don't you forget," Albert reminds Darcy, "It took three attempts in the legislature to secede from the Union and when it finally passed, it was only by a few votes."

"How dare you call President Davis a hothead," Darcy replies, raising his voice.

"Brown is the only intelligent governor in the South," counters Albert. "He is not letting the Confederacy take out men and materials to be squandered in some unknown part of the world."

Darcy's face turns red as the holly berries on the table. His left eye twitches uncontrollably. He knots his left fist in a ball until the blood drains from his knuckles. "That is blasphemy, you traitor."

"Traitor! Who is the traitor?" asks Albert. "What are your bank shares worth now? Inflation is ruining us. Do you know how much it costs for a pair of shoes?"

"All you think about is money," Darcy fires back. "Where is your patriotism?"

"Money, what do you know about money?" Albert's eyes cut through Darcy's glare. "All you do is sit in your bank and take our money and use it to make money. You have never worked for any money. I want to feed my family, not sing Dixie!"

The argument escalates. Finally, Mr. Robert steps between the two men. "Gentlemen, for the sake of Christmas, please stop this argument."

The two men walk away from each other and join their wives at opposite ends of the table. Seething with anger, Darcy picks up a wine glass. He holds the stem between his fingers and twirls the glass. The hot light from his eyes burns like the candles and reflects off the glass.

As if on cue, a legion of servers in starched white shirts and black trousers march in like a line of penguins and place on the table platters, tureens, bowls, and vessels of every description, filled with the widest assortment of food in the entire South, or so it seems to the guests. A large, roasted brown turkey and several platters of duck and chicken occupy the center of the twenty-foot mahogany table. Serving after serving is produced until all the food has been transferred from the kitchen to the sideboards and serving trays in the dining room.

Amos says to Amelia, "I have never worked as hard as today. How much food do you think we served?"

"Don't you worry about that," she responds. "You've got to help me with the dishes."

When the last fowl is devoured, a large glazed ham covered in brown sugar is taken to the table. Old James expertly takes a large carving knife and slices thick slabs to replenish the guest's plates. Mounds of vegetables, fish from the creeks and ocean, and relishes of all sorts disappear as hungry mouths lay waste to this movable feast, plate by plate.

Slowly small knots of guests grouped by age and gender move onto the veranda and continue their conversation. The old men tell stories rich in nuance and exaggeration—about General and Caty Greene, who built Dungeness; Cockburn cutting live oak and shipping it to Bermuda; the various skirmishes with the Indians who were unwilling to give up their land. The children listen intently, and believe all they hear.

In the evening, a dance commences at Planter's House. The guests dress in their finest linens: Union soldiers wear formal dress uniforms, and the women, who dance until dawn, float in their layered lace gowns. Six gaily dressed house slaves—Dido, Jack, Sam, Liberty, Brutus, and Gwinnet—play a variety of instruments, including banjo, fiddle, and tambourine.

Amos and Amelia are exhausted from serving and washing the mountains of dishes. They watch the festivities from the kitchen. The string of pearls that graces Missy Shetland's neck attracts Amelia's attention. The opulent river pearls glisten under the candle chandelier. She imagines herself someday in a similar necklace, wearing a large hoop skirt gown, dancing with a gallant gentleman. She taps her foot. Her head sways to the music. *But how will that happen?* she thinks. *I am a house servant ... who will want me? Look at my clothes, homespun and coarse, not like the silks worn by Master Robert's guests.*

But she remembers what Mammy Esther has told her. "Amelia, you are a fine-looking girl with grace and intelligence." That means much to her. *Perhaps I am,* she thinks. A broom stands in the corner. She grabs it and begins to dance.

"What are you dancing with that broom for?" asks Amos. "We got lots of dishes left." He interrupts her reverie. Then he calls out, "Hey Amelia, look at that. Master Darcy looks awfully mad. He is walking toward Master Albert with a cane."

"Albert, you seditious traitor!" yells Darcy.

Albert turns around to see Darcy holding a cane over his head, ready to strike. Quick as a fox, Albert throws a glass of wine in Darcy's face and simultaneously grabs the hand that holds the cane. Albert parries the blow. Both men swing at each other. The veins on Darcy's neck pop as his face flushes to a bright red. The anger that has simmered all afternoon boils over and overcomes his usual decorum. Out of control, he finds himself in the middle of a brawl in someone else's house on Christmas Day. Albert, the stronger of the two, pushes him outside and throws him off the veranda. Instead of having a sobering effect on Darcy, the cold air does the opposite. He is furious. Without his cane for protection, he can only defend himself from Albert's blows with his fists. He swings wildly at the other man. Albert lurches forward and drives his fist into Darcy's stomach. Darcy doubles over; he fights like a cornered raccoon trapped by dogs. Blood dripping from mouth and eyes swollen, the hate within him fuels his continued assault on Albert. But it is not enough. Albert is not only larger, he controls his emotions. After a few more blows, Darcy falls to the ground. Blood streams from his nose. The ground— not quite frozen, but cold enough—keeps the droplets of blood from leeching into the soil.

Mr. Robert and several Union offers run to him. "What is the matter with you?' Mr. Robert asks angrily.

"Albert's a Yankee lover!" Darcy exclaims. "And you might be too. Look at all these Union officers you invited, who contemptuously flirt with our women." Darcy wipes the blood from his nose and spits on the ground. He stands and glares at Mr. Robert.

"Darcy, given the circumstances, you will leave first thing in the morning," orders Mr. Robert.

Two days later, the slave celebration Jonkonnu begins. The celebration migrated to the American south from Jamaica early in the eighteenth century. Masked and costumed performers parade in the streets during the week between Christmas and New Year. Though Christmas is a religious celebration, Jonkonnu is a secular one. In Jamaica, three days—Christmas Day, Boxing Day, and New Year's Day—are set aside for free time. Jonkonnu is a safety valve that provides release from the repression of slavery and, as such, is supported by plantation owners.

Exhausted from Mr. Robert's celebration, the twins find themselves again helping in the kitchen. The extra ingredients their mom receives from the Christmas draw are used for special meals. Molasses, spices, salt, and meat are generously incorporated into the variety of dishes.

Beating drums signal slaves from all over the plantation to gather at the main slave quarters. The other plantation owners on the island give many of their slaves passes to attend the celebration at Mr. Robert's. Friends who have not seen each other for months embrace in bonds of warmth. Joyousness and gaiety permeate the gathering. The slaves are all dressed in the most unusual assortment of costumes; some dress like birds and others like animals. Brightly colored feathers and animal masks adorn the largest gathering the twins have ever seen on the plantation.

Soon, the birds and animals form into a long line to begin the parade. One's position in the parade is determined by one's social status within the slave community. The long serpentine procession that slowly makes its way toward Planter's House is led by the Ragman, respected for his wisdom in the slave community has strips of blue, red, green, and yellow cloth hanging loosely from his arms and legs. On his head, he wears a large raccoon headdress with two large, protruding ox horns. Through a skin pulled over his face, slits have been cut for his eyes and mouth. Strings of goat horns and several cow and sheep bells are attached to his elaborate costume so that he jangles at every movement.

A group of six richly costumed slaves dance behind the Ragman. Dressed in feathers, ribbons, and ornaments, they carry musical instruments called gumba boxes—sheep skins stretched on a wooden frame and beaten like drums to keep the performers in step. One performer, an older house slave named Thomas, wears one of Mr. Robert's old wine-colored jackets, blue-striped pants, and a black top hat with yellow hat band. His face is painted white.

Behind the leaders of this eccentric entourage march a large group of colorfully dressed women. Walking in teams and divided into all the colors of the rainbow, these women are "set girls." A white or brown mistress sponsors each set and takes great pride in her girls, showing them off to great advantage. Each team has its own queen, richly dressed and bedecked in the most expensive jewelry. These highly competitive team members will soon sing and dance, trying to outdo each other.

Jonkonnu is not just a holiday for slaves, it is also an opportunity for white mistresses to maintain or assert their status to each other. The competition between the patronesses is sometimes bitter. This anxiety regarding status is also reflected in the order of procession in the parade. Mulatto set girls dance ahead of the others. At the Jonkonnu festival at Planter's House, the rivalry is between the plantations on Cumberland Island. Since Mr. Robert is the most successful planter on Cumberland Island, he hosts the festival every year.

Because of the trouble Darcy Shetland causes at the Christmas dance, he does not witness this year's festival. He is not only an ardent secessionist, he is fearful of a slave rebellion. Earlier in the week, he admonishes Mr. Robert for encouraging Jonkonnu.

"Robert, you shouldn't let your people gather together during the holidays. You know them Negras, they get together and you don't what all they might do. I read the reports from Jamaica. Last Christmas, they burned buildings and terrorized the plantation owners. The authorities should outlaw that damned holiday."

"Darcy, that might be true," Mr. Robert replies, "but that's because their owners keep them on a tight leash. My people have a lot more freedom. I am more concerned about your white renegades on the mainland. The only people causing trouble here are those regulators."

"Never you mind, Robert," says Darcy. "If I were you, I wouldn't let my slaves gather for any reason. You are just asking for trouble. Jonkonnu gives them the opportunity, under the cloak of confusion, to do things they might never accomplish at another time of the year. With all the confusion and merrymaking, any one of your slaves could cause a lot of trouble, even burn property. It is a question of law and order."

Unlike Darcy Shetland, Mr. Robert recognizes the importance of Jonkonnu to his slaves and makes every effort to help them celebrate their holiday. He invites other planters to send dance teams to compete and provide additional entertainment. This year, unfortunately, only four plantations sent dancers. Several owners have left because of the war, and the others echo Darcy Shetland's concerns that the holiday will encourage a slave uprising. They are keenly aware of the slave rebellions that have taken place elsewhere.

For example, the most serious slave rebellion in Jamaican history, known as the Christmas Rebellion, erupted on December 27, 1831. Most of the planters have read Michael Scott's novel *Tom Cringle's Log* that describes "… the Kingston Regiment marching down to the court house in the lower part of town, to mount the Christmas guards … in case any of the John Canoes should take a small fancy to burn or pillage the town, or to rise and cut the throats of their masters, or any little innocent recreation of the kind."

Indeed, if that happens on the island, there are no Confederate troops to protect them. President Davis orders them to Tennessee at the beginning of the war. Several planters voice their opinions. They have no confidence that the Yankee soldiers assigned to the naval blockade will come to their aid in the event of trouble. Despite of their objections, Mr. Robert hosts the Jonkonnu celebration at Planter's House.

The guests assemble on the front veranda to witness the beginning of the celebration. The air rings with music. Banjos, tambourines, triangles, gumba boxes, castanets, and fifes contribute to the gaiety. Dancing, singing, and swaying, the procession winds its way around Planter's House. The Ragman leaps up on the steps and begs Mr. Robert for some coins, while the rest of the participants sing the "John Connah" song. Mr. Robert's guests throw pennies from the veranda.

Without warning the music abruptly stops. The dance teams separate from the crowd and move to opposite sides of the veranda. Everyone steps back to give them plenty of room. Four teams costumed in blue, yellow, green, and red form at each end of the veranda and wait for the music to begin. Mistress Lillian Lynch proudly waves a hand at her girls, dressed in red, and the competition begins.

The drums begin slowly as the red team members, arm in arm, move with the beat. As the tempo increases, other instruments chime in, and the girls separate and form a circle. The intensity of the drums and the quick movements of the dancers, first left then right, flitting like humming birds, dazzle the audience. Their feathered headdress sway like saw palms in the wind and keep beat with the music. All of a sudden, the music reaches a crescendo, and several dancers leap into the air as if propelled from a cannon. But they land softly. The bells and shells tightly wound around their ankles and wrists jangle as they dance ferociously. Beads of sweat roll down their long ebony arms, which glisten in the sun.

Team after team jumps into the circle. Each team dances harder and leaps higher than the one before. The onlookers sing and cheer. They encourage the dancers to perform more difficult movements. Mr. Robert turns to Old James. "Jim, I notice you and Mammy don't participate in the celebration. Why don't you join them?"

"Oh, they are just a bunch of showoffs."

"You think you are better than they are? "asks Mr. Robert.

"Oh, yes, sir. I sure do hope so."

9

Funeral

After the winter solstice, the year's shortest day, and the Jonkonnu celebration, the days lengthen in anticipation of spring. Persephone, trapped in the bowels of the earth after her abduction by Hades, soon will revel in the sunlight and bask in the flowering meadows again, as the Greek myth promises. The slaves, however, inured by bitter experience, are not as joyful. They drop the elegant mantle of joy and celebration that attends the holidays and replace it with the frayed cloak of cautious optimism.

Slaves and their white masters are vulnerable to diseases due to infection and poor nutrition. In eighteenth and nineteenth centuries, the East Coast of the United States—from the Barrier Islands to Boston—is ravaged by yellow fever epidemics. A tropical disease born in Africa and South America, the virus thrives in the holds of ships, like a stowaway. Any American port or coastal community can expect a visit from the Grim Reaper at any time. Once the yellow fever virus arrives, it soon reaches epidemic proportions as the virus is transmitted to man by mosquitoes. The Low Country, which, as its name implies, supports marshes, swamps, sloughs, and meandering estuaries, is a generous host to breeding mosquitoes.

The island will soon be alive. Lantana, broomsedge, and shepherd's needle will sprout through the decayed humus of the brown landscape and fill in the fields and roadsides. The understory, peppered with elephant's foot and sparkleberry, with its bell shaped white flowers, patiently waits. Tall magnolias sport shiny green leaves and pungent white flowers in the forest, standing in concert with hickory, sweet gum, and live oak. A cruel deception, the flowering spring masks the disease.

Due to the cold, winter brings other afflictions. In the North, the heavy white snowflakes that cover the ground after a late spring blizzard are called the "poor man's fertilizer." Cruelly, they remind one of nature's fickleness. April is the cruelest month. It can bring a late frost and kill the new growth. Children conceived in the spring will be born in the coldest month of the year. That's one reason the residents of Cumberland Island anticipate January with fear and trepidation.

A cold, black east wind sweeps the rain onto the island from the ocean. Ominous gray clouds scud across leaden skies. Rain pelts the roofs—not the gentle rain that softly runs down the gutters, but a ferocious rain that swells the sloughs in the inner-dune meadow and overflows the estuaries that flow into the marshes. The gale howls through the leafless trees. The small island deer and raccoons hole up in their lairs. The first storm since Jonkonnu keeps the slaves huddled inside their quarters.

Amos and Amelia open the door to their cabin. They stand on the doorstop soaking wet. Water drips on to the floor and puddles around their feet. They have just visited their mother, Zephia, at the hospital.

"Amos, is she gonna be all right?" Amelia asks.

"Sure she is," he replies.

"I don't think she looks good at all," Amelia says. "She complained all week about her back, said she was having awful cramps. She also has a fever and chills."

"Oh, I know. But most women who are going to have a baby say the same sorts of things."

"We've got to bring her some soup," Amelia says.

"When the rain stops, we'll run over to Mammy Esther and ask her to make some soup."

A few hours later, the rain subsides. Amos and Amelia run to the large summer kitchen, where Mammy Esther is cooking the late afternoon meal.

"What are you two up to?" she inquires.

"Can you make some turnip and pork soup for Mom? She is going to have a baby soon and needs her strength."

Mammy turns to the large plank table and cuts some pieces of pork and chops some turnip greens. She pours this mixture into a large black pot, adds water and salt, and watches it simmer as she continues to peel a large supply of sweet potatoes.

"It sure smells good," Amos says.

"How are we going to keep it hot in this storm?" Amelia asks.

"Don't you worry," says Mammy. "I'll give you this large cover to keep it hot until you get over to the hospital."

The twins let themselves out and head for the hospital. Though the rain has let up, the wind continues to howl. A brisk breeze forces them to keep their heads down.

"Boy, it's cold," says Amelia. "The wind cuts to my bones."

Mammy Esther watches the twins from the kitchen window. She is worried. *Lots of babies die in January*, she thinks to herself.

In the South, 51 percent of slave births result in infant mortality. Children die from a myriad of diseases—convulsions, lock jaw, suffocation, teething, tetanus, and worms. The Georgia and South Carolina coasts are frequently visited by yellow fever outbreaks.

Amos and Amelia enter the tabby hospital, one of the largest structures on the plantation. The bowl of soup is still hot and steamy when they carry it inside. The hospital is a two-story structure, divided into wards. The women are treated on the first floor and the men on the second. Each ward measures twelve feet by fifteen feet and has cots and a straw-filled mattresses. The floors are swept daily and washed weekly. Twice a year, the hospital is white-washed. The building includes a small kitchen and an examining room. On the coastal islands of Georgia, plantations with communities of seventy to three hundred slaves maintain substantial hospitals. Slaves who are ill are cared for and pregnant mothers deliver their babies. Nearby is another large building, the nursery.

Mr. Robert is keenly aware of the necessity to protect his slaves from the many diseases that afflict everyone in the South. He keeps a copy of *The Mariner's and Overseer's Medical Companion*, first published in 1807, and consults it often. Mr. Robert also employs Dr. William Bassest from Savannah to care for his slaves. Mr. Robert pays Dr. Bassest a set amount annually, and four times a year, the doctor visits the plantation and provides medical checks. In emergencies, such as accidents, he is summoned to set bones, stitch lacerations, and aid with fevers. Occasionally, he is called to assist with a difficult birth.

"Mr. Robert, your slave children are in good health. I don't see any 'dirt eaters,'" Dr. Basset says after his initial checkup.

"Dr. Basset, I take care my slaves. They eat well. I have been on the mainland where many children are malnourished. That's not the case here."

Mr. Robert's hospital staffs two full-time slave healers, midwives who not only perform deliveries but heal other aliments as well. Despite several laws regulating the medical practices of free blacks and slaves in the antebellum South, plantation owners allow slaves to administer health care, usually under the supervision of a white doctor.

An uneasy relationship exists between slave healers and white doctors. Slaves specialize in herbal medicines. White doctors do not. The primitive state of "professional" medicine contributes to black people's lack of confidence in white doctors. Many antebellum medical practices are not only ineffective, but dangerous. White doctors routinely bleed, cup, blister, and purge their patients, both white and black. In some cases they administer arsenic, lead, and mercury.

Slave healers possess specialized knowledge that the average slave does not have. They collect roots and herbs, make teas, and in some cases create charms to ward off evil spirits. This knowledge gives them special status in the slave community. Next to the slave preacher, slave healers are on the second rung of the social hierarchy. The midwives are the most intelligent women on the plantation. Their medicinal knowledge is passed down to them by older healers. They spend many hours in the fields and forests collecting and learning the various uses of roots, bark, leaves, and grasses—a skill that is revered in the slave community but reviled outside of it. Some slaves believe that their aptitude is an inborn, natural gift.

Mr. Robert is concerned about Zephia's health. He summons Dr. Basset to "be on hand." Zephia is pregnant and as large as a watermelon. She is not feeling well and is in the hospital. Hester, one of the healers, immediately recognizes the symptoms: Zephia is in labor. Hester brews a cup of cramp bark to relax her patient's muscles and ease the cramps. Just before the birth, she will brew a concoction of squaw weed, cotton, and horsemint for Zephia to drink. Hester knows that will speed labor. Zephia also has a fever. Hester is worried. The baby is in the wrong position.

Dr. Basses greets the twins. "You two be quiet. Your mother is resting. She will enjoy the soup."

Amos and Amelia quietly tiptoe into the ward. Their mother is sleeping. The ward has been scrubbed, and her bed has clean white sheets and a gray wool blanket. She lies alone. The twins leave the soup on a small stand by the bed, look at her, and quietly leave the ward.

"She needs her rest," Amelia says.

On the way out, Amos asks Dr. Bassest a question. "Is she gonna be all right, Doctor?"

"I'll know in a day or two. The baby is turned the wrong way; its feet are down. It needs to turn back; otherwise, she will face a difficult delivery. Hester has delivered a passel of babies, and I am sure that your mother will do just fine. When she wakes up, I'll be sure she eats the soup."

The rain that had turned to intermittent showers returns to the island in torrents, flooding all the low-lying areas. Amos and Amelia listen to the heavy drops pound the roof like a snare drum. Off in the distance, they hear the peals of thunder, which are followed by flashes of lighting. The low fire smokes, and the odorous smell of the ashes in the fire pit permeates their nostrils. The air is heavy with humidity. They sit together.

"I am glad Hester is with Mom," Amelia says.

"I am too," replies Amos. "She knows how to make people better. She has delivered many babies, and most of them get through the winter."

"I don't trust Dr. Basset," Amelia says. "He just wants to cut you up, make you bleed. Remember last year when old Miss Tammy was sick. He gave her some medicine and she died, but he blamed Hester. He said Hester's teas made her sick. Miss Hester makes everybody well. When Missy Lynch, Master Lynch's wife was pregnant, she asked for Hester. And Hester delivered a healthy baby boy."

"Hester has special knowledge," Amos says. "She is always out in the forest picking roots and bark from the trees. I see her talking with the older mammies when I do errands for Master Robert. They teach her how to brew teas and make poultices."

Dr. Bassest stays with Mr. Robert when he visits the plantation. Mr. Robert sits with a cup of coffee in the dining room, looking through the window at the rain. He taps the fingers of his left hand on the table. Dr. Bassest walks over to the sideboard and pours a cup of coffee into a white ironstone cup.

"Robert, I need to talk to you about Zephia and Hester," he says. "You know I don't approve of midwives delivering babies, particularly under these circumstances. They have no medical training. They have had no anatomical, physiological, or obstetrical training. Most of what they do is sheer superstition."

"That may be true, but all of my slaves love Hester," replies Mr. Robert. Her teas and medicines seem to work. Even Missy Lynch called for her last year when she gave birth."

Mr. Robert adds, "Dr. Basset, you are good at what you do. That's why I hired you to keep my slaves healthy. But you are only here when I call you. Hester, on the other hand, lives on the plantation and knows all the slaves and their families. They trust her."

"Robert, that may be so, but you can't tell me that sassafras and blood root teas can compare with professional medical training," the doctor says angrily. "For Lord's sake, your slaves think that haints live in trees!".

The next day, Zephia still has a fever. The baby has not yet turned. Hester tries several times to massage her stomach but to no avail.

"I'm going to give you some cotton root," Hester says to Zephia. "That will help speed the delivery." She makes medicines from red shank, cherry bark, dogwood bark, prickly ash roots, and black haw roots. In the event it is a prolonged birth, she brews birthroot, which speeds the process of labor. To ease the pain of childbirth she gives her patient calamus. Slaves are at ease with Hester because she understands their cultural beliefs and the rituals required to channel the supernatural forces for good rather than evil. She advises her family members and her patients about appropriate behavior at the time of birth.

Hester is well aware of a tragedy that happened two years before on a neighboring plantation. Mistress Susannah Bartow was born on the last day of March between midnight and daylight, when the moon was on the wane. At the moment of birth, a cold wind blew down the chimney and scattered ashes from the hearth. Tragedies befell the mistress—the sudden death of her mother and a daughter's elopement with a Yankee—all attributable to this single event. If only proper action had been taken, the family might have been saved.

Zephia burns with fever. Beads of sweat bubble on her forehead. Hester applies a cold compress. It doesn't seem to help. Zephia flails her arms. She throws off her blanket. She becomes violent. She complains of contractions. When she vomits, Hester is worried.

"Run, get Dr. Bassest," she orders a slave. "He's at the big house with Mr. Robert."

By the time Dr. Bassest got to visit Zephia again, she has been in labor for twenty hours. When he arrives, Zephia starts to hemorrhage.

"Quick, put some water on to boil," orders Dr. Bassest. He immediately administers ergot, a fungus found on rye, to relax her muscles in the hopes of restarting the labor pains, which had ceased.

"Hester," he says, "give her a tablespoon every three hours until she delivers. We've got to turn the baby."

"The baby doesn't want to turn," Hester replies.

Dr. Bassest looks worried. He has delivered children in the breech position before. The birth is hard on the mother and the child. Even if the birth is successful, the mother often dies a few days later due to complications. Internal injuries to the mother and hemorrhaging are a major problem.

"We'll have to take the baby." Dr. Basset rolls up his sleeves and wipes his hands on a towel. He does not wash them. Hester holds Zephia as Dr. Basset grabs the baby's feet and begins a slow pull.

Zephia cries an excruciating wail. After some time a baby boy emerges. Dr. Basset holds him upside down and slaps his buttocks. He cries. Zephia exhausted, lies limp in her bed. Beads of sweat roll from her forehead. Her nightdress is soaked with sweat. Hester cleans the baby, wraps him in a blanket, and places him on Zephia.

"Hester, don't leave Zephia for a minute. Let me know how she feels in a few hours. She needs to rest," said Dr. Basset.

It is a grueling birth for mother and child. Zephia lies exhausted. The baby, now clean, lies with her. Both sleep.

Hester speaks to Amos and Amelia. "Your mama is very tired, but the baby is fine. In a day or two she will be able to see you. You two go on home."

Amos and Amelia leave the hospital and return to Planter's House to do their chores. Mr. Robert waits for them. "How's your mama?" he asks.

"She's tired," whispers Amelia.

"We can see her in a few days," says Amos quietly.

The twins are uneasy and deep in thought. They don't look at Mr. Robert. They look at the floor.

Zephia's room is dark as a Roman crypt. The rain rolls off the hospital roof and plunges over the eaves like a cascade. Large washes of gray sky blot out the sunlight. The chilled air is damp. Wind blows from the ocean like shepherd's needle and penetrates to the bone. It is the coldest day of the year.

For the next three days Zephia lies still. Hester cooks broth and makes herbal teas. The weather delays Dr. Basset's return to Savannah. He stays with Mr. Robert.

"Robert, I am concerned about Zephia. She had a very difficult delivery and isn't responding well."

"Dr. Basset, you did your best," Mr. Robert says. "You are the best-trained doctor in South Georgia. Zephia is in good hands with Hester. It is now in our maker's hands."

The rain does not let up, and the wind continues to howl like a demon. In the early morning hours, Zephia lets life go. After her passing, the rain that has tormented the island with such vengeance abates. The western skies clear, and gentle breezes dry the island. Two nurses wash and prepare Zephia's body for the funeral. Elijah, a carpenter, builds a pine coffin. She is placed on a cooling board until the coffin is completed. This is the origin of the prayers that say, "Lord, I thank thee for permitting me to rise this morning and that my bed was not my cooling board." To keep her mouth closed until rigor mortis sets in, a nurse ties a piece of cloth under her chin. The other nurse places pennies on her eyes to keep them closed. When her body becomes stiff, she is wrapped in a sheet. For the next several days, family members and friends take turns watching the body, protecting it from wild animals. They pray and sing.

To a slave, the passage of the soul to another place is the climax of life. Death offers eternal freedom from bondage. Even slaves who are well treated, and Zephia is no exception, still want to be free. Slaves care passionately about their funerals and demand they are elaborate. Funerals reinforce cultural values brought from Africa. The rituals associated with funerals create a sense of community. Zephia's funeral will be a religious ritual, a major social event, because of her status, and a community pageant.

The sun sets in the west. The moon rises in the east. Purple hues wash the night sky. In front of Zephia's cabin, slaves drive six lit torches in the ground. Inside six slaves lift her coffin from the plank table and take it from the cabin. Many slaves gather around her coffin. Reverend Hale, a slave preacher, raises his voice in hymn. The mourners join in and sing:

> Steal away, steal away, steal away to Jesus!
> Steal away, steal away home,
> I ain't got long to stay.
>
> My Lord, He calls me,
> He calls me by the thunder;
> The trumpet sounds within my soul,
> I ain't got long to stay.

Green trees are bending,
Poor sinners stand a-trembling;
The trumpets sound within my soul,
I ain't got long to stay here.

My Lord, He calls me,
He calls me by the lightning;
The trumpet sounds within my soul,
I ain't got long to stay here.

During the antebellum period most slaves do not read or write. The few that do typically are house servants. Field slaves memorize verses of the Gospel and spirituals. The spiritual "Steal Away to Jesus" deals with what the Bible says and how to live with the spirit of God. Slaves often sing outside of church. Slaves were allowed to sing work songs when they were laboring in the cotton fields or cutting timber. In Africa, they sang in wooded groves.

Reverend Hale quickly leads into another song, one full of code that only the slaves completely understand. Hale leads the mourners in a call and response chant. He sings one verse, and the congregation answers him with another. The voices of the mourners surge in a mournful cadence punctuated by the intonation of Hale's next line:

Reverend Hale: *Swing low, sweet chariot*
Chorus: *Coming for to carry me home*
Reverend Hale: *Swing low, sweet chariot*
Chorus: *Coming for to carry me home*
Reverend Hale: *If you get there before I do*
Chorus: *Coming for to carry me home*
Reverend Hale: *Tell all my friends, I'm coming too*
Chorus: *Coming for to carry me home.*

To a white audience, the lyrics suggest home is heaven and are of no concern. However, to a slave, home also refers to the North or Canada and the sweet chariot is the Underground Railroad.

At the end of the song, an old slave recites from memory the biblical story about Jesus raising Lazarus from the dead, from the book of John, chapter 11. Everyone falls to his or her knees and listens to the old man.

"Now a certain man is sick, Lazarus of Bethany, the town of Mary and her sister Martha. It was Mary, who anointed the Lord with fragrant oil and wiped his feet with her hair, whose brother Lazarus was sick. Therefore the sisters went to him saying, 'Lord, behold, he whom you love is sick.'" The old man speaks with a firm voice that stirs the souls of the congregation. Amos and Amelia know the story well, but this time it gives them comfort. During the previous days they have cried themselves to the point that tears no longer can be shed.

"When Jesus heard that, he said, 'This sickness in not unto death, but for the glory of God, that the son of God may be glorified through it.' Now Jesus loved Martha and her sister and Lazarus. So, when he heard that he was sick, he stayed two more days in the place where he was."

The twins know that Lazarus is dead when Jesus says, "This sickness is not unto death." Jesus knew that Lazarus would be with the glory of God, not dead. They firmly believe that their mother is not dead, but that she with the glory of God.

"Jesus courageously decides to return to Judea and Jerusalem because he has put his trust in God," the old slave intones. "When Jesus reached Bethany, he found that the body had been in the tomb for four days. And Jesus spoke to Martha. 'Your brother will rise again.' Martha said to him, 'I know that he will rise again in the resurrection at the last day.' And as you all know, Jesus said to her, 'I am the resurrection and the life. He who believes in me, though he may die, he shall live. And whoever lives and believes in me shall never die.'" This is the promise of Christianity and is firmly believed by everyone at the service.

His final words were "Like Lazarus, call us your friends, stay in our company, share what we have, come to our aid when we call, and grant us eternal life."

Instinctively, the congregation rises to its feet. The pall bearers lift the coffin to their shoulders. Slaves hold torches high in the air, and in an orderly procession the mourners exit the cemetery. Spanish moss hangs like shrouds in the live oak trees, casting eerie shadows over the mourners as they travel the worn path to the cemetery. A night owl flies silently over their heads on his nocturnal rounds. In the distance, a mourning dove whistles its plaintive melody. The congregation in a mournful wail sings "Sometimes I Feel Like a Motherless Child." The serpentine procession sways in unison with the rhythmic movements generated by the soulful music and the flickering of torches. Drummers accompany the songs of sorrow, keeping the marchers in line with the slow beat of death. With death so close, the mourners feel the presence of haints.

The grave is dug, the dirt still damp from the torrential rains. It is a placed in an east–west direction. The pall bearers put the coffin in the ground with Zephia's head to the west so her eyes can face Africa. She is gone. Her soul departs, and she is with God. Before the grave is filled, a small child is passed over the coffin. This is to ensure that Zephia's spirit is sealed before her journey.

The drummers beat their drums, and the mourners raise their voices in song:

> Before I be a slave
> I'd burn in my grave
> And go home to Lord
> And be saved
> O, what preaching
> O, what preaching
> O, what preaching over me, over me
> O, what mourning …
> O, what singing …
> O, what shouting …
> O, weeping Mary …
> Doubting Thomas …
> O, what singing
> O, freedom …

When the song is over, each person throws a handful of dirt into the grave. Reverend Hale walks to the head of the grave, raises his hand over the congregation, and speaks: "The hour has come when we must part from you. What the earth has decreed, we cannot help. We have done for you what we could. We have given you a funeral worthy of you. You must care for us, and you must deliver us from all evil that may come upon us."

It is over. The pageantry, the strong sense of community, and the religious ritual that binds the slave community together has concluded. The mourners raise their voices in song, depart the gravesite, and disperse into the darkness like apparitions. Amos and Amelia stand at the edge of the grave tightly holding hands. Tears roll down their cheeks. They listen to the plaintive melody of the mourning dove. They are alone. A great sadness, like the incoming tide, washes over them.

10

Letter

News of the war slowly flows to Cumberland Island like a meandering estuary. The Union blockade has effectively prevented Southern shipping from reaching its destination. Not only is the flow of supplies—food stuffs, medicines, and ammunition vital to the Confederacy—interrupted but newspapers and letters are as well. This slow strangulation has devastating repercussions throughout the South. Like a boa constrictor, it slowly squeezes all communication in the region, creating hardship for military planners and civilians alike. The newly invented telegraph clicks out news and dispatches instantaneously, as long as the lines are not cut to newspaper and government offices on the mainland. This is not the case on Cumberland Island. Mr. Robert, like other planters on the barrier islands, patiently waits for news to arrive.

All islands, regardless of their economic or social institutions, are isolated, surrounded by the sea, and Cumberland is no exception. In the antebellum period, the only means of communication is by boat. News from European capitals often takes months. News from Northern newspapers is often nonexistent. Although Mr. Robert has business interests in Connecticut and banking relations in New York, even messages to him arrive several weeks late.

The Confederate States Army wins decisive victories in the early part of the war, beginning with the First Battle of Bull Run. This war, like no other war before, uses technology in a way that was never conceived before and creates new standards of warfare that will be used well into the twentieth century. The Battle of Bull Run takes place late in the afternoon; a fresh supply of Confederate soldiers arrives on the field to create a major Union rout. General Johnston transports them by rail from the Shenandoah Valley, the first time in military history troops are moved by train. The soldiers who already there are fatigued after marching many miles and fighting all day in excessive humidity and soaring temperatures; the infusion of fresh troops tip the balance, and the Yankee soldiers quit the field. It is ironic because later in the war, trains will prove to be a decisive element in the defeat of the South. The North builds rail lines at an unprecedented pace—ultimately ten miles of track for everyone in the South. Bull Run is the dress rehearsal for the war, which will be a long and difficult, brutal, and have tragic consequences that no one can foresee.

Jefferson Davis, a secessionist before the war and the newly elected president of the Confederacy, appoints Robert E. Lee to command the army of the Confederate States of America. Lee selects a highly skilled group of subordinates, including Stonewall Jackson, Jubal Early, and James Longstreet. They unleash a series of victories that alarms the North. Until Antietam and Gettysburg, hopes run high in the South for ultimate victory. Victories in the East, primarily Virginia, are enthusiastically celebrated, but Confederate planners become increasingly anxious about developments in the West.

A relatively unknown soldier, unremarkable at West Point, unable to qualify for the artillery or engineering corps, is relegated to the infantry. Major General Ulysses S. Grant is the son of a tanner, a recently promoted captain who fought in the Mexican War and whose drunkenness causes him to resign in semi-disgrace. He wins the Union's first battles of the war—the Battle of Fort Henry on February 6, 1862, and the Battle of Fort Donelson on February 16, 1862. Within two months, Admiral David Farragut, commander of the Union Navy, captures the city of New Orleans. This is the beginning of the western strategy to control the Mississippi River and split the South in two. Lincoln looks for a general who can win battles, and Grant is that general. He will command Union forces and move south toward Vicksburg, the crown jewel of the South. As long as Vicksburg stands, the South can continue to fight. Meanwhile, Farragut sails his fleet north up the Mississippi River and disrupts supply depots and forts along its banks.

The war, with the exception of the Union blockade, not only seems far away to the residents of Cumberland Island, it *is* far away. Other than the fracas with the regulators, who are arrested and imprisoned, little suggests a war is being waged. The island lacks the deprivations, runaway inflation, and the letters from the front informing loved ones about the death of a husband, father, or brother. Like the ocean which surrounds the island and keeps it safe as a geographical defense, the planters live in a bubble of security, but that bubble will soon burst and usher in the harsh realities of the struggles on the mainland.

From the time the war begins, Mr. Robert spends a lot of time gazing through the window in deep thought. His mind seems as distant as London or Paris. One afternoon, Amos and Amelia are polishing silver in the pantry, a chore neither one enjoys.

"Look at this!" Amelia says with a groan.

"Yeah, I know," Amos complains. "This silver gets black as fast as we polish it. Seems like that's all we do is polish silver."

"What's wrong with Master Robert?" Amelia asks.

"Oh, he's all right," Amos says. "Probably concerned about business. Everything is stored in the sheds. He can't sell anything, although, yesterday his face lit up like a shiny star when the mail was delivered."

"Why?" Amelia asks.

"I handed him a pile of newspapers and letters from the mail boat. He sifted through the bundle and selected one. He read it, folded it, and put it in his vest pocket. 'Amos,' he said, 'It's a fine morning.'"

Amos and Amelia continue to polish the silver and make plans to meet Tom later in the day. They will fish for mullet late in the afternoon. They are as unaware as everyone else in both North and South of events unfolding in Washington City, which to Cumberland residents seems as far away as London or Paris.

President Lincoln convenes a meeting of his military leaders to consider a scheme proposed by Commodore Porter, who has just helped Farragut take New Orleans. Secretary of the Navy Gideon Wells and General George B. McClellan are present. Abraham Lincoln produces a map and with an outstretched finger says to his staff, "See what a lot of land those fellows hold, of which Vicksburg is the key." He picks up his pointer.

"Here is the Red River, which will supply the Confederates with cattle and corn to feed their armies. There are the Arkansas and White Rivers, which can supply cattle and hogs by the thousand. From Vicksburg, these supplies can be distributed by rail all over the Confederacy. Then there is the great depot of supplies on the Yazoo. Let us get Vicksburg, and the country is ours."

Lincoln walks away from the map and into a shaft of sunlight coming through the window. He let his generals gather around the map like bees in a hive to ponder this possibility.

"The war can never be brought to a close until that key is in our pocket. I am acquainted with that region, and I know what I am talking about." He turns to his aides and looks at each man in the eye. "We must take Vicksburg!"

As a young man, Lincoln traveled by flatboat down the Mississippi and knows exactly what he was talking about. The military leaders present are astounded by the civilian president's grasp of the situation. Commodore Porter later remarks, "A military expert could not more clearly have defined the advantages of the proposed campaign."

Amos and Amelia put the gleaming silver into the walnut cupboard, turn the wooden lock, and leave the pantry. "Boy, I am glad that is over," Amos says. "Let's go fishing."

Amelia notices Mr. Robert's vest hanging over a chair. She picks it up to put it away when a letter falls from it and to the floor. On the back of the envelope, over the wax seal, she reads:

Private Armand Stafford
26th Regiment
Groton, Connecticut

"Amos, who is Armand Stafford?" Amelia asks.

"I don't know, maybe a relative," he remarks casually, more interested in fishing than reading somebody's mail.

Amelia returns the letter and places the vest back on the chair. Her mind flits like a hummingbird around a yellow and orange lantana plant. *Who is Armand Stafford?* she thinks to herself.

Amelia runs to the door and gives it a push. Outside, shadows from the live oaks race across the meadow. The sun, low in the sky, still warms their faces. They run to meet Tom. It is early summer, and the spiderwort with its clusters of blue flowers dots the meadow. Tom is waiting, as usual, with three fishing poles. To get to the beach, they cross through the maritime forest with its loblolly pine, gum trees, and live oaks. The forest creates a canopy that keeps them cool. Once into the dune meadow, they brush against buttonweed, muhly grass, and seaside goldenrod.

Tom yells out, "Watch out for the devil's joint. Those spines are prickly and will stick you."

"Oh, I know," says Amos, "I got stung last year running through here. Let's get to the beach and catch some fish."

Amelia's mind swirls like seaweed in a tidal current. Still thinking about the loss of her mother, she can't stop wondering who Armand Stafford is. Why does Mr. Robert keep Armand's letter in his vest pocket but leave all the other mail on the secretary?

The tide is almost full. Long, low breakers break gently. Bubbles of foam roll up onto the beach. Terns stand along the shoreline, like passengers waiting for a ship to dock. Oystercatchers, with their red beaks, skim the crest of the waves. Sea gulls screech and fight for any morsel that lies on the beach.

"Toss your lines!" Tom yells. "It's going to be a good day." All three cast their lines into the sea with a splash; soon they are standing mid-thigh in the water.

"Amos! Who do you suppose Armand Stafford is?" Amelia asks once again.

"I don't know," he replies. "Why don't you ask Mammy Esther? She knows everything and everybody on this island."

By the time the shadows from the sand dunes intersect with the outgoing tide, Amos, Amelia, and Tom possess a mighty haul of mullet.

"A good catch," Amos says. "Let's get home and clean them."

The next morning Amelia's curiosity can no longer contain itself. Mammy Esther is in the summer kitchen preparing the mid-morning meal. The smell of grits, ham, and biscuits fresh from the oven fills Amelia's nostrils as she opens the kitchen door.

"Mammy Esther, do you know who Armand Stafford is?" she asks.

Mammy Esther, startled, stops rolling out dough. She catches her breath. "How do you know about Armand?"

Amelia explains that she's seen his name on the back of the envelope.

"There are some things you folks don't need to know about," Mammy Esther said. "But I guess the horse is out of the barn." She picks up the large wooden rolling pin and starts to roll out the dough. She throws some flour on the dough to keep it from sticking to the pin. Then she cuts the dough into rounds with an old glass jar and looks straight into Amelia's eyes.

"Life doesn't always turn out the way it's supposed to or the way you want it to," she says. "A long time ago, Zabette, a person who became my very best friend, lived up at the Bernardy plantation. She was a beautiful woman, a mulatto. Some of my people called her a 'yellow gal.' Well, just like you and Amos."

Although Amelia hasn't thought much about the color difference between her and Mammy before, it becomes crystal clear now that it is brought to her attention.

"When Master Robert's mother was sick, just before her death, Mrs. Bernardy sent Zabette, a slave and a well-trained nurse, to care for her. In gratitude, Master Robert asked her to take over the household duties of his plantation. At the time, we never knew what arrangement Master Robert had made with Mrs. Bernardy, but it sure caused trouble later."

"What kind of trouble?" Amelia asked.

Mammy Esther slides a baking pan full of dough circles into the oven. She slowly walks over to the larder, grabs a large cured ham, and sets in on the large plank table. Taking a large knife from the cutlery box, she carves thick slices of ham and arranges them on several large platters. Mammy Esther is in no hurry to tell the story, while Amelia is frustrated by what seems to be an eternity. She asks again, "What kind of trouble?"

"As soon as Zabette took over the duties in the big house, we became good friends. It wasn't long before she told me how much she liked Master Robert. I was shocked. Servants don't mix with their masters or mistresses. I told her not to get involved with Master Robert. 'Nothing will come of it, and you will be the center of a major scandal.'"

Amelia's eyes are big as a full moon. The idea of Mr. Robert with a slave is outside the realm of her imagination. What was he thinking? What was she thinking? Everyone knows a very clear line separates the races. This news explodes like a bag of flour falling off a shelf.

"Well, do you want to hear more?" Mammy Esther asks, as she continues to prepare the mid-morning meal.

"What happened to Zabette?"

"She had a baby, Mary," Mammy replies. "That's when the trouble for her started. Her mother screamed at her and most likely beat her for getting pregnant with a white man. She was furious that her daughter broke the code between white and slaves. She knew that gossip and tales would pass between plantation slaves like a torrential downpour. And she also knew that this relationship didn't ensure her protection. Zabette put herself out on a limb. If it broke, no one would take her in."

"Where is Zabette today?" Amelia asks.

"She is up in Connecticut with her children. You see, Master Robert loves his family. A few years after Mary was born, Robert and Armand followed in line. And, as it turned out, Master Robert was very considerate of Zabette. He sent them to Connecticut to protect them."

Throughout the South during the antebellum period, marriages between whites and "persons of color" are not only unrecognized, they are illegal. At a time when the "caste system" prevails in the South, the following designations are ascribed to non-whites: creole, metic, mestico, metis, mustee, Negro, free Negro, people of color, mulatto, tri-bloods, slaves, maroon, and nominal slave. It is clear that white society wants a clear separation of the races. Zabette, described as both a mulatto and a "person of color," could not have come forward to claim her share of Robert Stafford's estate, even though she is his common-law wife. Such an action is unthinkable before the war. Slaves have no right to own property. After the Emancipation Proclamation and the end of the Civil War, her status as a slave effectively disappears. However, she is still a person of color, a physical fact no law can eradicate. After the war, when the state constitution is revised, the Georgia State Supreme Court rules that the section of the black code prohibiting miscegenation is not invalidated by the new clauses. According to the court's interpretation, Zabette's children are not only illegitimate, they are also the offspring of a Negro. In nineteenth-century Georgia, Negro children have no legal status.

Mammy Esther turns to Amelia and says, "Master Robert loves Zabette and his children. He knows exactly what he is doing. To be direct and honest in this state is not to be safe."

Amelia thinks about this: to be direct and honest is not to be safe. "So, we are not to tell the truth, Mammy Esther?"

"Honey, there are many rules. Some are made by men and not always fair. Then there are God's rules. I think, Master Robert lives by God's rules. He is truly in love with Zabette. So, to answer your question, the truth depends on whose rules you choose to follow."

There is a timelessness in agricultural communities. Nature determines its own rhythms. The slave's workday and type of work is determined by the rising and setting sun and the seasons of the year. Days gently side into months and months into years. Special events and holidays are duly noted and celebrated, but most of the time, time meanders like a slow-moving stream. Summer is the slowest season of the year.

A red ball of fire slowly rises over the ocean, foreshadowing another stultifying July day. A Bermuda High settles over the southeastern Unites States, and the hot spell continues. The cycle of convection storms begins later in the day when the torrid heat soars to thirty thousand or forty thousand feet and collides with cold air in the upper strata. Condensation results, and clouds form that create great thunderheads, some with anvil tops. The ominous and potentially violent clouds, black with fury, produce short-lived torrential rains. These convection showers saturate the air and increase the already uncomfortable humidity. The air in these storms is as full as a sea sponge, with not a wisp of wind to offer the smallest relief.

Mr. Robert rocks on the veranda in his favorite rocking chair and reads the newspaper. His Panama hat, sweat-stained and rumpled, lies on a small table beside him. He pulls a handkerchief from his pocket and wipes his brow. He feels the sweat slowly drip down his arms. A cicada chirps, followed by several more, a sure sign of a hot day.

"When do you suppose this heat will let up?" he asks Amos, who is coming onto the veranda with a large pitcher of spring of water.

"I don't know," Amos replies. "I don't ever remember it being this hot for so long. Even the afternoon showers don't give us a break."

"Amos, the war seems to be taking a turn for our side," says Mr. Robert. "The paper reports that on July 4, General Pemberton surrendered Vicksburg to General Grant. Robert E. Lee's army was defeated in Pennsylvania at a town called Gettysburg. This means that the war will soon be over."

Amos listens carefully to Mr. Robert. How does he know that the war will soon be over? Vicksburg? Gettysburg? *Where?* Mr. Robert has taught Amos and Amelia how to read but not about geography.

"Amos, the Union is like a ghost crab; it has two pincers. Vicksburg is caught in one and Gettysburg in the other, and the Union is about to squeeze them together. Ole Jeff Davis is meeting right now with his generals to determine the terms of surrender."

Mr. Robert is dead wrong on this count. Southern armies are besieged on all fronts; General Bragg is in full retreat in Tennessee; Port Hudson, commanded by an unpopular General Pemberton, is under siege; and federal troops attack the barrier islands off Charleston, South Carolina. However, Jefferson Davis has no intention of giving up.

"We are now in the darkest hour of our political existence," he tells his cabinet. But "now we have less territory to defend." Instead of accepting the bleak reality and surrender for peace, which in the long term will be in the South's best interests, he decides to continue the fight. The Confederacy teeters on destruction—that is the reaction of Davis's generals. Jefferson Davis's sense of reality is clouded by the decisive victories General Lee achieved against lesser and more timid generals than General Grant. In the early battles of the war, Lee defeated McClellan, Pope, Burnside, and Hooker. Davis and Lee have not yet encountered Union commanders like Grant and Sherman, generals who fight battles from the same tents and bedrolls as their men. Unlike "office generals" who remain detached from their units in the comfort of palatial homes and who drink expensive imported wine, Grant and Sherman are fighting generals.

Like a late afternoon convection shower, the war is soon to explode with all its fury and darkness on Mr. Robert's veranda. As Mr. Robert explains the war to Amos, he recalls the details of the last letter he received from Armand in early February.

Dearest Father,   January 17, 1863

I hope this letter finds you well on the island. We sailed from Connecticut to Brooklyn, New York, and then to the Gulf of Mexico. It was a long passage when our regiment finally arrived at Camp Parapet. Several of us got seasick, but we are finally back on land. Camp Parapet is north of the city of New Orleans on the Mississippi River. It was a joy to see Admiral Farragut's ships as we sailed past to reach our destination. The rebels built the camp, and we are using it to train for an upcoming battle. We were issued weapons in December and knew we would soon be engaged in the fighting, though at this time no one seems to know where or when.

The camp is located on a flat area with few trees. I suspect the rebels cut them down. The clay is red and very muddy when it rains. Our major enemy is disease; several of my friends have contracted malaria and typhoid. About 25 percent of the regiment is on sick bay. So far, I am well. I share my tent with eight other soldiers from Groton. We have a wooden floor and bunks, so not much to complain about. The rations are good; fresh bread is baked daily, and the commander lets a sutler in to sell us vegetables in the morning. Our morale is good, but we are all ready for a fight that is soon to come. I'll write again soon.

Your son, Armand

Mr. Robert then turns his attention to the description of the war he's given Amos. It is possible that Armand is in the fight for control of the Mississippi River. Beads of sweat roll off his forehead. The spring water in the glass is tepid. A few flies buzz around his head.

"Amos! Snap those flies; we don't need them around here," he says.

Amos quickly grabs a swatter and chases after the flies. Three swats later the veranda is quiet again. The air is still. The heat pushes the sweet sour pungent smell of grasses, flowers, decaying matter into their nostrils. Amos is first to notice the mail boat approaching the dock.

"Master Robert, that boat will have news," he says.

"Amos, run down to the dock, and get whatever they have. It's too hot for me to be running around."

Amos leaps off the veranda and sprints for the dock. The captain hands him a large army haversack and says, "This is for Mr. Robert. I think it is sad news."

Amos carries the haversack over his shoulder. There is a letter attached to the outside addressed to Mr. Robert Stafford, Planter's House, Cumberland Island, Georgia.

Mr. Robert slides his pen knife across the top of the envelope and opens the letter. He sits very quietly for a long time. His jaw tightens. A tear forms in his left eye and slowly rolls down his cheek. The letter reads:

Dear Mr. Stafford,

Your son, Private Armand Stafford, died bravely fighting for his country at the siege of Port Hudson on June 16, 1863. We are sending you his personal effects.

Sincerely,

Dr. Asbel Woodward, Medical Director
26th Connecticut Regiment

"Amos, open the haversack and pull out what is inside," says Mr. Robert. Amos pulls out several unsent letters tied together in a bundle and hands them over. Mr. Robert slowly opens the first letter and begins to read.

Dearest Father,   May 23, 1863

Yesterday, early in the morning with the rising sun in our eyes, we arrived by steamer at Springfield Landing. The entire regiment disembarked about six miles north of Port Hudson. From the bow of the steamer, I could see and hear mortar shells arcing over our heads and exploding into the city. I saw the fortifications for the first time. Port Hudson is located on a bluff overlooking the Mississippi River. It became clear to me why our boats are having so much trouble. The river makes a bend at this point and slows down any river traffic. The cannon batteries control the river. Although I cannot see the defenses on the east side of Port Hudson, we have been told that the Confederate commander, General Gardner, constructed rifle pits, redoubts, salients, and breastworks to fortify the city. On our march toward the city, I noticed a series of natural barriers that will make our fight difficult. The area surrounding Port Hudson is full of ravines, swamps, and gullies overgrown with lush vegetation. Magnolia forests, tangled with vines and underbrush, give the rebels real good cover. All around us, as we march to our camp site, Union forces are amassing. Regimental flags from Vermont to Michigan to New York are all snapping in the breeze. I have never seen so many soldiers in one place. Soon the battle will begin.

Your son, Armand

A blood red sun rises over the Mississippi River. "Red sky at night sailor's delight; red sky in morning sailor's take warning" serves as an omen of the battle rather than the weather on the morning of May 27, 1863. The 26th Connecticut Regiment assembles outside the defenses of Port Hudson to mass one final assault and victory. If successful, particularly after General Grant's siege of Vicksburg to the north, Union forces will control the Mississippi and Red Rivers and effectively cut the Confederacy in half.

Now is the time. General Godfrey Weitzel amasses his troops on the north side of the city. At 10:00 in the morning, his men are about a quarter of a mile from enemy lines when the order is given to advance. In close formation, shoulder to shoulder, men step off. A long blue serpentine line slowly moves forward, unit flags flying and music playing. Soon the lines—which were so well organized in quick order drill, marking time and arranged with precision on the parade field—find themselves in chaos as they enter the ravines and gullies. Confederate sharpshooters fire relentlessly from behind trees and fallen logs. As wave after wave of blue keeps coming, the rebels give ground and retreat to the defenses of the city. Union forces reach a clearing.

Across a treeless landscape—the trees were purposely cut by the Confederate States Army to create an open field of fire—Union troops anxiously reorganize for the final assault. Confederate fortifications lie about two hundred yards away. Weitzel's men stop in their tracks. An explosive execution of .527-caliber British Enfield rifles, canisters, and grape shot from a well-aimed fusillade slow the assault. At any given time in a maneuver like this, sixty thousand deadly projectiles will shower a field. Canisters consists of loads of iron balls the size of marbles that spread a field of fire like a shotgun at oncoming soldiers. The mini ball from a rifle or canister can rip through flesh and splinter bone. Anyone hit is disabled.

———⟆ᴓᴓ⟆———

Dearest Father,   May 28, 1863

I just survived my first major encounter with the enemy. At about 2:00 in the afternoon after much delay, we formed our lines on the east side of Port Hudson. For several hours we could hear and see smoke from the north side of the city. Seeing all that smoke and hearing the loud thunderous roar of cannon, I was a bit scared but did not tell anyone. Directly in front the 26th was the 6th Michigan Regiment and off to our left was the 128th New York Regiment. In the woods off to our right, the 15th New Hampshire was forming its lines. It turned out to be a very warm day, and we suffered terribly from the heat. Many soldiers were pointing to the north. I looked in that direction. Great black billowing clouds of smoke rose over the field.

The bugle blew. We were one of five regiments ordered on double quick and began the assault. Wave after wave of bluecoats advanced toward the southern and eastern defenses of Port Hudson. Several fence lines disrupted our initial charge. Our regiments became entangled with one another; confusion reigned. Almost immediately, the Confederates unleashed a barrage of fire that threw men to the ground, the lucky ones. The ones on their feet were slashed with grape and canister shot. I learned later in the day that General Sherman was shot in the leg and taken off the field. I saw Colonel Kingsley, who led our charge, fall to his knees almost immediately. Blood was flowing from his face. The explosive reports of cannon and rifle fire set off concussive waves that stunned many soldiers; some fell dead, never being shot, with blood draining from their ears. The crashing of nature's thunder could not compete with the thunderous punctuations of the Napoleons, Parrotts, and mortars that were hurling steel at one another. The Confederates used their defensive position to their advantage. All around me men were down, some dead and many wounded.

Our advance was slowed. Directly ahead of me was a parapet that contained a nest of rebel soldiers. A trench dug around the parapet was filled with water. I volunteered with about thirty other soldiers to form an advance storming party. A group of colored soldiers with poles and planks to make a bridge lined up with us. We waited for the 1st Vermont Battery to send a barrage of shot and canister to clear the parapet. The cannons went off and before the smoke had cleared, we charged.

We charged with bayonets at their position. All of a sudden, they opened up with a blinding musket volley. Our battery dared not fire because we were in front of them. In the melee, balls whistled around our heads like hornets, and many men went down. We were pinned down between our battery and their parapet. Several of us crawled to a ravine for cover and continued to fight for about another hour. The rebels were well dug in. We never got to the parapet and were ordered to retreat. We did not want to retreat and continued to shoot but to no avail. Captain Stanton got within about twenty yards of the parapet, stood up in defiance of the rebs, and got shot in the head. He died on the spot.

We suffered heavy losses but are determined to take the city. Morale is high, and soon victory will be achieved. Tomorrow we plan a full scale assault on Port Hudson.

Your son, affectionately,
Armand

—⟨⟨⟨—

Mr. Robert sits listlessly in his chair. The humidity presses his shoulders like an anvil. He falls into a great depression. Tears flood his eyes. He looks out across the sound. Armand's death brings back the terrible loss he felt when he lost his mother. Ironically, he sent Armand to Connecticut to protect him because of his color, and he is killed in battle as one of the first colored casualties fighting for the Union cause.

11

White Deer

A three-day blow lashes the island. It is a black, hard, driven rain. Great breakers of white and green foam rush onto the beach and into the inner-dune meadow. The water spills around the island and rips saturated soil from the banks. Trees with large roots topple into the sound and are swept away with the high tides. The island's animals, including the deer, hole up in their lairs.

When the wind backs around to the west and the skies clear, Mr. Robert calls out into the kitchen for Amos and Amelia.

"Hey, you two, go find Tom! I have a task for you to do today," he says. "I'm sure this storm washed up debris from the ocean. Some of it might be useful. Certainly driftwood will be good for fires. Sometimes line or boxes of cargo from ships out to sea will wash ashore in a storm. I want you three to start down at Dungeness, walk the shoreline back here, and bring back what you find."

They are overjoyed. It means a break in their routine in the kitchen—no more scrubbing and cleaning, at least for a while. Their imaginations blaze like flames. They think about what they might find. The possibility of adventure lies ahead.

Amelia yells out, "Let's race to Dungeness! You two can't beat me." Before any one answers, they sprint down the road trying to avoid the large puddles.

"Look out!" Amos screams "That one is really big." It is too late.

Tom is not able to jump over it. With a large splash, he trips and falls right into the middle. He is soaked from head to foot. Amelia laughs first, then Amos, and finally Tom.

"Don't worry. You'll dry off in the sun," Amelia says.

The tide is low and exposes a strip of shoreline that hugs the bank. Three sets of footprints emerge as they searched for any item of value the storm has washed ashore. A large beech lies across their path, its limbs submerged in the water, its gnarled roots pointing skyward.

"Let's just climb over this," Tom yells.

They jump onto the large trunk and grab its limbs for balance. Then, one by one, each jumps onto the narrow strip of sand. Scanning the beach ahead, they see nothing of value. The beach narrows and forces them close to the bank, whose walls are wet and cool. Roots poke out at them.

Suddenly, Amelia speaks up. "Look at the bank. What's stuck in there?"

They all look carefully and begin to pull shards from the bank. Mud covers the pieces, still, it is clear that the objects are manmade. But how old are they? Amelia is first to wash her pieces in the sound. She holds several pieces of broken clay in her hands. Embedded in each one are mysterious designs.

"What do you suppose these are?" Tom asks.

'I don't know, but they look like broken pots or bowls," Amos offers.

"Who would bury them this deep?" Amelia asks.

"Let's take them back to Old Jake," Amos says.

"Old Jake! He's as old as the trees," Tom yells.

"Yeah, but he knows everything about the island," Amos replies.

Holding their newfound treasures, they can't decide whether to go back the way they came or climb the bank and cut through the woods to find Old Jake.

"Let's cut through the woods. It's much quicker, "Amos says.

They scramble up the bank and into the forest. Amos and Tom know this part of the forest well. They always travel this way to fish. Great droplets of water rain from the trees. Tom, who is almost dry, complains that he is getting wet again. Suddenly, off to their left, Amelia glimpses a movement. She gently touches Tom's arm and motions him to stop. Amos does too. Three deer stand motionless with ears straight up, peering at them. Every so often one of the deer flicks its tail, flashing a spot of white against the green background. It is a standoff: the three deer and the three children watch each other. A branch snaps, and a small white fawn emerges from a thicket. Ghostlike, it ambles over to the adults. In stark contrast to the deer, the fawn shines like a bright light. Then with a crash, they all bound off into the forest, their white tails waving like flags in a parade.

"Did you see that?" asks Tom.

"I have never seen a white deer," answers Amos.

"Me neither," says Amelia.

They are puzzled by and think the deer must be magic. Now they have two questions to ask Old Jake: Who made the mysterious pottery shards? And are white deer magic? As they walk through the forest, they feel like they are on a mystical journey. While in the past they'd think haints might come down from the trees and grab them by the throat, today magic is a positive force.

Old Jake sits in his quarters on a worn, polished chair, swishing flies with a palm frond. His face is the color of soft cinnamon. His hazel-green eyes stare across the room. The veins on the back of his hand are blue and spidery, separating like rivers at the mouth of a delta. White frizzled hair curls over his ears. He sits stoically, looking through the window, rhythmically swishing the frond, deep in thought.

"Hey Jake!" the children call.

He is startled by the noise. "Who's that?" he calls out.

"It's us. Amos, Amelia, and Tom," Amos replies. "We found some old pieces of pottery with magical designs and saw a white deer."

"A white deer?" Old Jake thinks for moment.

'Yes! Out in the forest. We have never seen a white deer."

"I've got a story to tell you, but first let me get a drink," Old Jake says. "Come, sit outside under the magnolia tree. The shade will cool us."

Old Jake stands up and walks slowly to the water bench that sits outside in the shade of his cabin. His left foot drags slightly. The dipper hangs on a hook next to a bucket full of clear spring water. He bends over, clutches his fingers around the handle, and scoops a dipper full of water.

"Here, you have some too," he offers. "When I was your age, I crossed through the forest. One day, I saw a white deer, just like you. I asked my grandfather if the white deer was magic. And he told me this story:

"Many, many years ago, a long time before our time, a great tribe of Indians lived on the island. They were Timucua. They had a legend about a white deer. Over four thousand years ago, they erected a large village called Tacaturo. For them, the island was an ideal place to live. Tacaturo was similar to many other Indian communities that dotted the Florida and Georgia coasts. These people had a fishing-hunting-gathering society and flourished until the Europeans arrived, the people who brought us here. They ate oysters, raccoons, whitetail deer, black bears, gray squirrels, and rabbits, the most plentiful of all. The natural landscape provided a wide variety of native plants that thrived in the forest, including oak and hickory nuts, persimmons, grapes, and black cherries. They used large wooden spades to cultivate a large number of crops: maize, beans, pumpkins, gourds, cucumbers, citrons, and peas. They used weirs and spears to catch the fish. It was an ideal place to live."

Amos, Amelia, and Tom have never heard that other people lived on the island and are full of questions. Old Jake's mind is a labyrinth of memories and events, each one locked in a different room. To unlock each door and reveal its contents, they have to ask a question. Amos, Amelia, and Tom fire questions like shots from a Navy Coly revolver.

Amelia asks, "What did they look like?"

"The Indians were sturdy, muscular, and athletic and stood more than seven feet tall," Old Jake says.

Tom's eyes get really big. "They must have been giants," he says.

"They had olive and tawny complexions and hawked noses. The women rubbed bear grease into their skin and used other emollients and cosmetics that made them look lighter colored than the men. Both the men and women grew their hair very long. While the women let their hair flow naturally to their hips, the men dressed theirs on top of their heads, entwined with mosses and vines. They also used their hair for quivers for their arrows, which were tipped with a poisonous mixture of deer blood and rattlesnake venom. Both the men and women had long, pointed fingernails, which they used as weapons. They pierced their ears and wore inflated fish bladders and decorative pins made from shells."

"Boy, they must have scared their enemies," Amelia says. The others agree.

"You all know how warm it is here," Old Jake continues. "Unlike us, they wore very little clothing. The men wore loin cloths made from deerskin and saw palm, and the women wore apron-like garments of Spanish moss, smoked over aromatic fires. Both men and women wore girdles, painted red and fringed. Their ornaments were made from feathers, shells, and animal teeth fashioned into necklaces, ear pins, and bracelets."

The three sit, mesmerized, in the shade of the trees. A cool breeze rustles the leaves.

"Their families were called clans. Each clan tattooed itself according to rank: the chiefs and their families used red, azure, and black paint dyes, applied with black needle rush from the marshes. As symbols of friendship and mutual respect, they presented decorative deerskin cloaks and bird plumage to their friends."

Their imaginations are fired by Old Jake's story. They can't imagine large, feathered, tattooed people.

"They had a chief named Tacaturo, just like the village. As chief, Tacaturo had a large house with special seating platforms as well as a council house. He was greeted with both hands raised twice the level of the head, palms open forward, while the greeter intoned, 'Ha he ya ha.' Others present then chimed in with 'ha.' The chief was tattooed and wore many shell beads and ornaments of highly prized copper from northern Georgia."

"Ha, he ya ha … ha he ya ha," Amos says. "Ha he ya ha," the others chime in. They all laugh.

"These early people were very religious and considered the supernatural to be part of the natural world," Old Jake says. "To them, religion was a part of everyday life. As a result, no special day was set aside for religious worship. Their religious leaders were called shamans. They had a great deal of power. One of their primary obligations was to prepare the black drink, cassina, for ceremonies and medical purposes. They roasted yaupon holly leaves over a fire, after breaking them into smaller pieces, and put them in ceremonial containers with water. They would heat the containers, filter the tea, and drink it served in shell cups in the council house."

"That must have tasted horrible," Amelia says, rolling her tongue around her mouth.

"That isn't all," says Old Jake. "The Indians who drank black drink vomited and sweat profusely. You see, cassina contained a high level of caffeine, which caused hallucinations. They used it in religious ceremonies and to prepare for battle. The shamans presided over hunting ceremonies—intoning chants over deer disguises used as camouflage for deer and turtle hunts and a special bundle of sticks, which were used as fire drivers. In return for these prayers, the shaman was given the first animal killed. The Timucua were superstitious and believed in omens."

"You mean, like haints?" asks Tom.

Amos looks disgusted. "I told you, Tom, there ain't no haints."

"Yes, there are. They live in trees," Amelia blurts out, defending Tom.

"Let me continue," Old Jake says. "For instance, if a hunter who killed the first deer ate the meat, lungs, or liver, bad luck would follow the next hunting party. They cleaned animal bones and hung them around the dwellings, near the thatched roofs, to bring good luck. The first fish caught in traps, called weirs, were released for the same reason. They also believed omens could be conveyed by animal behavior, dreams, or natural phenomena. Lightning was a sign that warfare would soon occur. Whistling could prevent canoes from overturning in rough water. A bleating fawn caused nosebleeds and death. The song of a blue jay meant someone was coming to visit or an event was about to occur. So you see they were very superstitious."

"How do you know so much?" Amos asks Jake.

"I listened very carefully to my grandfather and I asked many questions," Old Jake responds. "Then I would tell the same story to myself, over and over."

"What else did he tell you?"

"Lots more. For instance, these Indians were traders and established a trade network that extended to the Ocmulgee Mounds near what is now Macon, Georgia."

Amos has heard Mr. Robert talk about Macon, but has never heard of the Ocmulgee Mounds. He knows Macon is far away and that it must have taken many days to get there.

"They traded seashells from the island all the way to north Georgia in exchange for copper," says Old Jake. "Beads, shell gorgets, and other ornaments were often used for barter. Indians in the Carolinas would give the Timucua three or four dress buckskins for a well-made gorget."

"How did they know where to go?" Tom asks.

"Oh, they followed the old trails made by the buffalo. They also took advantage of the rivers that flow from the interior of the state. They crossed large rivers in rafts and they made dugouts from cypress, poplar and pine to navigate the longer stretches of the rivers. Whether by foot or water, trade goods flowed from the interior to the coast and from the coast to the interior. Coastal Indians traded salt-dried fish, seashells, and the leaves of yaupon holly—the same plant used in the black drink—for red ocher, red root, flint, hard cane, feather cloaks, pottery, and animal skins from the interior. Inland Indians prized conch shells because they could be used as dippers and trumpets. Soapstone, copper, mica, and wood for making bows were frequently traded as well.

"You know the shells you collect on the beach, the lettered olive shells?" Old Jake asked. "Those shells were highly prized by the inland Indians. The pattern on each shell is unique, and the early Indians believed they were made by departing souls. The Indians not only traded with the Indians from the mainland, they also traded with the Europeans when they arrived. Until this time, the Timacua had led a peaceful existence on the island. What they did not realize was that the three different groups of Europeans—Spanish, French, and English— were competing for the same land. This led to war and the eventual downfall of the Indian culture. It is terrible to think about what comes next in this story."

Old Jake's voice becomes soft, and he speaks in measured tones. It is as if the tide has changed and the water is receding.

"Early in the sixteenth century, the Spanish explored and settled the Caribbean Islands. They searched for gold, silver, and minerals. They cut timber, mined minerals, and established plantations with slaves—Indians captured during raids along the Florida and Georgia coasts. When Juan Ponce de Leon made landfall on the Florida Keys in 1513, he found the inlands denuded of all natives, due to the earlier slave raids. He sailed north to Florida. A year later in 1514, slave-raiding parties from Santa Domingo ravaged Indian villages in coastal Florida. Most of the five hundred slaves they captured died before they reached Hispaniola. The Spanish relentlessly combed the coast from the northern Timacua territory to its southern boundaries in search of slaves," Jake's voice remains soft.

"Gold and silver? Here?" exclaims Amos. "I didn't know we had gold on the islands around here."

"We don't, but the Spanish thought it existed and in the process of searching for it destroyed lots of people," Jake says. "But it wasn't only the Spanish that caused trouble. The French soon followed the Spanish. In 1550, French explorer Jean Ribault sailed with a crew of 150 and established contact with the Timacua. He sailed past Saint Augustine to Cumberland Island and then on to South Carolina. The following year, another explorer, Laudonniere, sent explorers into South Georgia and built Fort Caroline on Cumberland Island. The French thought they had a stronghold here, but they were wrong. The Spanish destroyed both the fort and the French fleet in one decisive blow. By 1556, Saint Augustine was a well-established military post and the seat of Spanish rule. From this stronghold, the Spanish attempted to convert the native population to Christianity with the cross and the cross-bow."

"The cross and the cross-bow?" the children ask. "What does that mean?"

"It means that the Spanish wanted to convert the Indians to Christianity, but they weren't able to do it with reason, so they resorted to military action. The Indians wanted to retain their own religious system. Beginning in 1582, a tribe of Indians, the Guale, rebelled several times, but by 1590 they had been subdued. While the Spanish built missions and converted Indians, the French engaged in trade. French sassafras traders came and went unhindered. When steeped in boiling water and made into tea, sassafras brought relief to sick sailors. It cured headaches, colds, lameness, and constipation, but probably its most important function was the cure of venereal disease. The Spanish mission of San Pedro (Cumberland Island) became the sassafras trade center of the New World and was even larger than the presidio at Saint Augustine. The safe harbor at Cumberland's South End became the most popular marketplace for Spanish and French traders.

"Spain sent Jesuit priests to pacify the native population and encourage them to maintain peace with the Spanish forces. The mission of San Pedro de Mocama was built on the south end of Cumberland for this purpose. The natives were organized into a labor force to build a church and other buildings needed by the priests and soldiers. Spanish law permitted colonial leaders to take *repartimientos* which included rights to land and the use of native labor. Many of these same natives became soldiers and were used to capture slaves. These early policies were not well received by the native population and the Timucua rebelled. In fact, they were many revolts, but let me tell about one in particular.

"On seeing the outrages to which the Spanish subjected the Indians, one chief, Tarihica, started a rebellion, in keeping with the emperor and absolute lord that he'd been when they were pagans. Even though they were now Christians, many chiefs and leaders still recognized Tarihica as absolute ruler. The revolt started with an insult, for which the friars blamed the governor. He insisted that the native leaders carry their own provisions, telling them that Spanish sergeant-majors and captains had done the same on occasion. Tarihica refused to send his tribal leaders to Saint Augustine bearing cargo like ordinary Indians. Incensed by the governor's order, twenty-three Indians went on a killing spree. They burned buildings and killed many Spanish soldiers, officials, and colonists, they did not burn churches or kill friars. This was because the friars supported the Indians and defended them to the king, explaining that while the Spanish were used to carrying out such orders, the natives were not. Nothing in their value system had prepared them for such instruction."

Amos has a puzzled look on his face. He seems to be thinking.

"What are you thinking about?" Old Jake asks.

'It doesn't make sense to me. Why would the people of the cross not agree with the people of the cross-bow?" Amos asks.

"That's a good question," responds Old Jake. "It's because one group wanted to conquer souls and the other wanted to conquer land—two different goals, two different approaches. Well, let's continue this story.

"The Spanish then tried to replace the Jesuits with another religious order, the Franciscans. Recruiting Franciscans was difficult; many deserted service before their ships left Spain or jumped ship when they docked for resupply. Only two in twelve destined for missionary service in the New World ever arrived.

"Once the mission site (*doctrina*) was established, churches and residences for the friars were built. Initially, native and military labor was conscripted to construct the missions. Haciendas, or large farms, were also established in various areas; they provided wheat, corn, and cattle for the military and for export. The Spanish introduced new agricultural products, including watermelon, peaches, figs, oranges, garbanzos, sugar cane, pomegranates, garlic, cucumbers, barley, cabbage, lettuce, and wheat. Chickens, pigs, and horses were imported as food and as pack animals. These foods and other goods were gifted to the chiefs in return for cooperation.

"The Timucua were organized into a series of clans. Clan membership determined the status of an individual and a family. The Spanish were very clever. They exploited Timucua clan membership for settlement purposes. When the Spanish realized the White Deer clan was accorded the highest status, they exploited it. They gave heirs of the White Deer clan special educational opportunities. Children were removed from the villages and sent to board with the friars in mission schools. Shamans, on the other hand, were discredited as pagans, and the Spanish cast doubt on their skills with herbal medicines. In this way, the chiefs became dependent on the Spanish, not only for goods, but for the status and respect they needed to maintain their positions. The chiefs were the first to be baptized, and they convinced other natives to convert to Christianity."

Tom, whose mind seems to be wandering, because he is drawing designs in the dirt with a stick, suddenly looks up. "Jake, was that the same clan the magical white deer was named for?"

"I believe so," answers Jake. "You see, the Indians were superstitious. Because the white deer, like the one you saw earlier, was so rare, they believed it held special powers. The combination of religious conversion and exploitation allowed the Spanish to use natives as conscripted labor for agriculture, domestic service, and construction. They unloaded ships; built roads and bridges; acted as servants to friars and soldiers and their families; transported goods from Saint Augustine; hunted, fished, and worked the fields; and provided all services and food required by the mission. Native labor built Castillo San Marcos in Saint Augustine, a project that took adult males from their homes for months. For this, they were paid in goods. Over three hundred workers on the castle received two sizes of hawk's bells, knives, blue glass beads, multicolored glass beads, a razor, cloth, scissors and pieces of sheet brass for their months of labor. They traded these goods to other Indians for hides and other useful items. The Spanish then acquired the hides as vails (signs of submission) to the mission."

Old Jake sits quietly for a few minutes, swishing the flies with his palm frond. Amos, Amelia, and Tom try desperately to absorb all this information. Jake leans forward in his chair, looks intently at the three, and continues his story.

"The Timucua were a proud people, even though they submitted to Spanish domination and were indeed slaves. The worst was yet to come. Epidemics invaded the villages like no army could. Small pox spread like lightning strikes on the island. Within days victims whose faces became red with rashes saw the rash move to their arms and legs. Over 80 percent of infected children died from the disease. Smallpox is highly contagious and is transmitted from person to person. The Indians who lived together in communal villages were vulnerable to the infection.

An entire village could be wiped out in one outbreak. These epidemics continued year after year.

"Other calamities also had an impact on the Timucua. Violence erupted all along the east coast. Mainland missions were moved to the barrier islands to protect local natives from other tribes. The Chichimec Indians, who migrated south due to the Iroquois wars, were enlisted as slave raiders by the English, who armed them and sent them into Georgia. By 1657, the Guale had been decimated by these raids, and the survivors joined the Timacua for protection. The Chichimec raids into interior Georgia forced inland tribes to relocate on the coast. These wandering tribes were called the Yamasee, which means northern. When the *doctrinas* at San Pedro (Cumberland) and Santa Maria (Amelia Island) were abandoned, the Yamasee inhabited the islands. The Spanish used them as *repartimientos* (labor) in exchange for military protection.

"By 1670, the English had settled Charles Town, present-day Charleston. The Carolinian English supported the slave raids of the Chichimecos, who continued to attack Spanish settlements for native slaves in Saint Simon's and Saint Catherine's. Males were sold in Charles Town, but thousands of women and children were used as human shields against Spanish attacks before they were sold. By 1700, more than twelve thousand natives had been moved out of Florida, leaving north Florida and southern Georgia without most of their native populations.

"During the early 1700s, French and English pirates raided the barrier islands. Missions were sacked and then burned, which forced residents to move north, seeking protection from the English. In retaliation, the Spanish attacked and virtually wiped out all the remaining Indians on the Georgia coast. Amid slave raids and pirate attacks, epidemics of diseases rapidly spread through native populations. Smallpox was spread by African slaves. In one measles outbreak, more than ten thousand natives died. Workers sent to Saint Augustine took back infections routinely. Mission populations were consolidated to conserve laborers, which spread disease even more. Ten generations after the landing of Ponce de Leon in Florida, only one in fifty Timucua Indians survived in the region. The Spanish governor in Florida ordered all missions from

Cumberland Island northward abandoned. A culture that flourished for over two thousand years was destroyed in less than 250 years. The Timucua were gone forever.

Amos, Amelia, and Tom are stunned when Old Jake finishes his story.

Old Jake says, "This island has seen a lot of violence, devastation and disease—all brought on by Europeans. The Timucua were a generous people and would give away their goods because they placed no value on the accumulation of wealth; the worst thing they could be accused of was stinginess. This was not the case with the French and Spanish. The Indians compared the Europeans to a cougar. The cougar, they said, is an animal that will sometimes kill two deer at a time, more than it can possibly eat, and yet will lie between the two carcasses, too greedy to share its surplus."

Amos, Amelia, and Tom leave Old Jake filled with new knowledge about the island. "Before we saw the white deer in the forest we knew nothing about the people who lived here before us," Amos says. "It is a place with a sad history. An entire race of Indians destroyed and now this terrible war."

Subdued, they walk slowly to Planter's House and their evening chores.

12

Aftermath

The war is over. Church bells peal the news throughout the North and South. The yoke of slavery is broken. Slaves on plantations raise their voices in song: "free at last, free at last." Like a phantom that rides furiously in the night sowing seeds of destruction, the end brings chaos to Planter's House.

The previous Christmas, General Sherman presents the city of Savannah to President Lincoln. This event has little effect on the residents of Cumberland Island. Southern resistance, though seriously imperiled, is not yet over. More battles are fought. The carnage continues until General Grant accepts General Lee's sword at Appomattox Court House.

Cumberland Island and Planter's House are spared the ravages of war that many Georgians endured during Sherman's march to the sea. But now the war is over. In January 1865, the Sea Island Circular Sherman's Special Order 15 states that "islands from Charleston south, abandoned rice fields along rivers for thirty miles back from the sea, and country bordering St. Johns River, Florida, are reserved and set apart for Negroes now made free ..." Black people living in the now-former slave quarters on Cumberland Island expect to receive deeds to their property. However, in May, President Andrew Johnson issues the Amnesty Proclamation, which pardons most Southerners and restores property rights. Abandoned lands are divided into forty-acre lots and leased to male heads of freed families at an annual rate of 6 percent of the appraised value in 1860. Freedmen can enter into contracts with property owners.

This policy is not successful on Cumberland Island. Thirteen of the former plantations had been abandoned, and their owners do not return after the war. One former owner, Phineas Miller Nightingale, returns to his property, Dungeness, but only to use the mansion for a summer house. Nightingale prefers to let his fields go to ruin than to have strange Negroes squatting idle on his property. Most freedmen go to Fernandina which is overcrowded and rife with disease.

The euphoria that explodes after the surrender at Appomattox soon turns ugly on the island. Early one morning, after boiling coffee for Master Robert, Amos steps onto the veranda for some fresh air. The sky is dark. He hears a loud commotion off in the distance.

"Master Robert, who are those people coming our way?"

"Renegade slaves, I suspect. They are sailing from Fernandina. They want our plantation," Master Robert replies.

Amos shudders. He recalls a Bible verse from church, Isaiah 13:5. "They came from a far country, from the end of heaven, even the Lord, and weapons of his indignation, to destroy the whole land."

"Amos, where are Amelia and the baby?" asks Mr. Robert. "Go find them. And get them back here!"

"She's with Mammy Esther. I'll be right back." Amos stares out the window. The sky is still dark. He remembers Isaiah 13:10: "For the stars of heaven and the constellations thereof shall not give light: the sun shall be darkened in his going forth, and the moon shall not cause light to shine." He is very anxious. *Is this an omen?* he wonders.

Amos slips out the backdoor and under the cover of darkness runs like the wind to the summer kitchen. Carried by the wind, the voices catch up with him. He bursts into the kitchen.

"Amelia, get the baby and run back to the main house. Master Robert is upset!"

"Go, honey! Don't keep Master Robert upset," Mammy says.

"What for?" What's going on?" Amelia asks.

"Don't ask any questions. Just do as I say!"

Amelia picks up the baby. She clutches it to her. He begins to cry. Amos and Amelia step into the cool early morning air. She covers the baby's head. The marauders do not see them as they run back to Planter's House. A cacophony of voices splinters the early morning air. It frightens the baby, who begins to wail. Amos and Amelia enter through the backdoor and take refuge in the house.

Mr. Robert sits on his rocking chair on the veranda, his rifle in his lap. With the war over, most of the Union ships have sailed away. Only a small detachment of Yankees remain. They are overwhelmed by the lawlessness that creeps over the land. Mr. Robert can no longer rely upon their protection.

The renegade band warily approaches the house. Mr. Robert rises to his full six-foot height. He stands above the renegades. Each has a club in his hand. Ten against one, except Mr. Robert has a rifle: a standoff.

"One more step, and I'll start shooting!" he bellows. "No one will take my property."

The former slaves do not expect resistance. All of the other plantations on the island are vacant. They fully expect to divide Mr. Robert's property into parcels. Instead, they find a defiant man, a gun, and a voice of authority that throws them into a panic. They disperse quickly. Some run; others back away slowly. Mr. Robert hears the baby crying in the main house.

"Shush, little baby, don't you cry … We'll be okay today," he says.

As the sun rises in the East, it casts a reddish glow over the landscape. Amos watches the gang of former slaves disappear like apparitions into the wall of trees. Master Robert has driven them off his land.

"Will they come back to harm us?" Amelia asks. She is not usually frightened. But now she has her baby brother to care for.

"I'm not sure," Mr. Robert says. "I don't think they expected us to be here. All the other plantations have long since been abandoned. But if they come back, I'll be ready." Mr. Robert turns from the veranda, walks into the house, and puts his gun into a glass gun cabinet.

"Why are we having all this trouble?" Amelia asks.

"The war is over," says Mr. Robert. "Since the surrender of Appomattox we have been under the yoke of General Sherman's Order

15. Slaves who were recently freed have been given parcels of land to farm from their former owners, that is, if their owners left their plantations before or during the war. I did not leave. Therefore Sherman's order doesn't pertain to me. However, the men I drove off this morning believe they can take my property."

"Somebody better straighten this out soon," Amos says.

"I have spoken with military authorities in Savannah to seek relief. They have assured me my land is mine. The trouble is, no one else seems to know it."

The terror of the morning subsides. Amos walks outside and stands on the veranda. The dark shadows that crept across the fields dissipate as the sun rises. The red glow evaporates. Amos can clearly see the barren cotton fields and maritime forest. The early morning hues of red are brilliantly clear. He can see every tree but no people. He turns toward the twelve brick slave cabins, which sit empty, lifeless. Since the end of the war, slaves have been leaving the plantation to seek their freedom. Except for a pileated woodpecker that lands in an oak tree, nothing or no one is in sight. *Perhaps we are safe?* he thinks.

The empty slave quarters startle Amos. *What if their occupants don't return?* he thinks. *Who will work the plantation?*

Mr. Robert has acres of cotton in cultivation and several stands of loblolly pine and hickory waiting to be cut. For the first time in his life, Amos's thoughts move from the present to the future. This unsettles him. Until this moment, he has been comforted knowing that, no matter what events rain on Amelia and him, they will always be safe with Mr. Robert.

Like a waterfall cascading with crashing fury, his thoughts reel with uncertainty. His head aches as he walks into the house. Posed like a Mathew Brady photograph is Mr. Robert. He sits in his chair, Mammy Esther stands behind, and Amelia holds the baby straight and tall on his left. His future stands before him.

Though Master Robert has driven the fugitive slaves from his property, it takes a great deal of strength. He looks old and slumps in his chair. Wrinkles, heavy with wisdom, accentuate his forehead. Gray curls loop over his ears. His speech slows when he speaks and is followed by a sigh. During the past few years, the spring in his step has uncoiled. He moves with measured steps.

Mammy Esther, too, seems frail. Once a woman with robust energy and organizational skills, she too moves slowly, though she retains a twinkle in her eyes. When Mammy sits down in a chair beside Mr. Robert, Amos sees an old white man and an old black woman, who appear as bookends. These two, each in their own way, have kept Amos and Amelia on a straight path with love, affection, and expectations. Old Jake is gone. Tom is gone too; his family took him to Fernandina.

Amos looks at Mr. Robert and Mammy Esther. His mind swirls like eddies in a frothy stream. "Master Robert, how do you feel?" he asks.

"Fine, Amos." he replies. "I'm just a bit tired. It's been a long morning."

"Mammy, I think Master Robert needs another cup of coffee."

"I'll get it!" Amelia offers.

Amos paces back and forth on the Oriental rug.

"What's gotten into you?" Mammy Esther blurts out. "You will wear it out walking that way."

Amos turns quickly. His eyes flash. "We've got a problem! The fields lie in ruin, timber isn't being cut, the canals are filled with silt, and strangers from the mainland are trespassing unhindered on our plantation."

Shocked by the outburst, Mammy says, "Amos, shut your mouth. We don't speak that way in front of Master Robert."

Master Robert sits up in his chair and leans toward Mammy. "Amos is right," he says. 'I have been thinking about our situation for some time. When the slaves left for Fernandina, we lost our work force. I am not going to contract people I don't know to help me run this plantation."

"Master, what are we going to do?" Mammy asks.

"Mammy, you will stay with me and do what you have always done. Our time is soon coming, and we will be fine until then," Mr. Robert says.

Amos is stunned. Amelia gives him a quick glance of bewilderment. The air, warm and humid, suddenly feels like a white-hot fireplace poker. The tension of the last few weeks explodes like a rifle shot.

Amelia speaks first. Caring for her baby brother has helped her develop the protective instincts of a mother bear. "What about us?"

Thoughtfully, Master Robert turns toward her. His crystal blue eyes gaze into hers. "The baby needs to be cared for. He needs a family and it takes more than one person to raise a child. You will need help. Mammy and I are too old," he says.

Quick as always, Amos realizes what Master Robert has planned for them. On the north end of the island, a group of former slaves have started a settlement. The land is unclaimed. Dido, who helped save many slaves during the devastating hurricane, is their leader. Amelia, the baby, and Amos will be safe in the north end.

"But we have been here all our lives. What are we going to do?" Amelia asks.

"Though no one planned for this to happen, you are both prepared to make a new life away from the plantation," Mr. Robert says.

"You children have overcome a lot these past years," Mammy says. "The hurricane and the war with all its uncertainties have made you strong. Just a few years ago you were playing on the beaches and in the tidal pools, fishing in Big Pond, and getting into trouble with your old friend Tom. Look at you now, all grown up."

A quite hush covers the room like an old worn quilt. All know but do not speak of it. The death of Amos and Amelia's mother is still too fresh in their minds.

Master Robert changes the conversation. "Amos, I've got a problem you need to help me with," he says.

Amos, always ready to help, says. "You can depend on me. What is it?"

"I want to burn the slave quarters."

"Burn the slave quarters?" Amos is bewildered by this request. "Why the slave quarters?" he asks.

"All my slaves have run off and I don't want strangers squatting on my property. I can't trust them. They might destroy our sheds or kill livestock. There's no telling. If there is no shelter, they won't move in here," Mr. Robert says emphatically.

Amos feels Mr. Robert's rage rising like a swarm of angry hornets.

"I treat my slaves well. I built the hospital and nursery to care for the sick and newborns. Each Jonkonnu I give every man, woman, and child new clothes. No one on this plantation is mistreated. And now, with the bell of freedom ringing loud and clear, they leave ... to go where?"

His anger, disappointment, and frustration boils in an emotional cauldron. He looks at Amos, his eyes wild with anger, and wags his finger. "Burn those buildings!"

For the next several days, Amos keeps a sharp lookout for any freed slaves from off the island. He takes Mr. Robert's buggy and patrols the road to the south end of the island. Mr. Robert's demonstration earlier apparently has frightened them, for Amos does not see any signs they are still on the island. He waits for the wind to die down. If he has to burn the cabins for Mr. Robert he does not want to start a major grass and forest fire. The next day the air is still and humid. Amos can smell rain.

"Master Robert!" Amos calls. "Today is a good day to burn."

After the surrender of Appomattox, General Robert E. Lee finds himself homeless, as are many of his soldiers and fellow citizens. The war destroys the South. It will take many decades to recover. Radical Republicans do not want General Lee to forget the war. They confiscate his ancestral home, the Curtis-Lee mansion that overlooks the Potomac River and Washington City, and consecrate it as a national cemetery for the Union war dead. Today, it is Arlington National Cemetery. Shortly after the war, Lee takes a sojourn south to visit Fort Pulaski and Cumberland Island.

After his visit to Fort Pulaski, General Lee sails to Saint Mary's. He arrives late in the afternoon. The following morning, the sky is clear and the humidity from the previous day has been swept away by a brisk west wind. Sea gulls circle and screech as he walks to the dock. He sees an old gray-haired black man mending nets, his fingers nimble and worn like the nets themselves. Lee approaches him.

"I want transport to go over to Cumberland Island. Is anyone living over there?"

"Yassir. Old Master Robert lives at Planter's House. His dock is in good repair. It's the only place you can safely land. Except for some freed men and their families who live on the north end, the island is deserted."

At Planter's House, Mr. Robert reads the newspaper in the cool of the morning.

"Master Robert, here's your coffee," Mammy Esther says cheerfully.

"Thank you!" he replies as he takes his first sip. "Good coffee, Mammy."

He looks up quickly. Something catches his attention. It is a white sail. After a few minutes, he realizes it is headed straight for his dock. *Who might that be?* he thinks. Since the end of the war and the departure of the Union fleet, there has been little maritime traffic. He grabs his cane and takes the well-worn path to the dock to greet this unknown visitor.

Robert E. Lee stands at the bow. He pulls his gray frock coat over his shoulders as the west wind blows his gray hair. Though it is early fall, the brisk wind chills his bones. Planter's House suddenly appears behind the magnolias and oaks of the maritime forest. *What a magnificent structure*, he thinks. The semitropical gardens shout their color, a fusion of floral diversity. This scene stands in sharp contrast to the burned hulks of buildings and ravaged farmlands he's witnessed during the war.

"Welcome to Planter's House!" an elderly gentleman calls out to Lee. "Sir, I am Robert Stafford."

"And I am Robert E. Lee."

Both men shake hands. The two Roberts meet—one a wealthy Union sympathizer, the other a famous Confederate general.

"What brings you to Planter's House?" Mr. Robert asks.

"My father was "Light Horse" Harry Lee. He died when I was young. I understand he is buried on this island."

"Yes, he served with General Nathaniel Greene during the Revolution," Mr. Robert replies.

"I want to visit his grave."

"I will show you the way. But you mustn't be discouraged. Dungeness, where he is buried, is in disrepair. The war has taken its toll ... Amos!" Mister Robert yells. *What's wrong with me*, he thinks. *Amos is gone.*

"General Lee, wait right here. I will drive you." Mister Robert pulls the buggy and two tackies to the main house. General Lee gets in slowly. With the crack of a whip, the two pull onto the main road, a drive Mister Robert has taken hundreds of time. The live oaks draped in Spanish moss shade them from the sun. General Lee is intensely interested in the variety of birds and wildlife that dart in and out of the forest.

"What kind of bird is that?" he asks Mister Robert, pointing to an iridescent blue bird high in a hickory tree.

"A neotropical," Mister Robert replies. "That little one is from West Africa. Sometimes they get caught in the upper winds and are blown west as far as this island."

They emerge from the forest into acres of barren fields. Weeds have overtaken the cotton fields like a wartime cavalry charge. The borders of the fields are filled with loblolly pine and scrub oak, which compete for sunlight. The soil has not been turned, weeded, or hoed for years.

"Before the war, this was a prosperous plantation," Mister Robert says.

"As was much of the South," General Lee says.

Mr. Robert pulls the reigns hard right, and the buggy turns onto a path that leads to Dungeness plantation and Harry Lee's grave. A large white tabby structure looms before them. It badly needs whitewash. Derelict in its despair, both men feel the enormous weight of the war's consequences.

"This is what our nation has done," Mister Robert says solemnly.

"And I fear the worst is yet to come," General Lee replies. "We have created a whole new population of freedmen with a very tenuous future."

Mister Robert thinks about Amos and Amelia. Both intelligent, they have many skills. He had taught them to read. He knows they can manage a plantation, but the plantations on the island lie in ruins. Their owners have left. The economy is destroyed. Has the war destroyed their future?

The two men walk to the gravesite. Hats in hand, respectful of "Light Horse" Harry Lee, they stand in quiet reflection. A simple white marble stone rests in a grove of magnolias to mark the grave.

"My father fought for freedom and liberty," Lee says.

"And, we both embraced the ideas of freedom and liberty," said Mr. Robert. How then did we fight such a tragic and destructive war?, he thought to himself.

He leans on his cane. He feels old, as his thoughts carry him to his past. The evacuation of Fernandina and the Union naval blockade leaps forward in his mind. It is there that Amos and Amelia are introduced to violence and chaos. Within months, his cotton shed burns to the ground, but he savors the satisfaction arising from his capture of the culprits. The annual Christmas and Jonkonnu celebrations provide a respite from the weariness of war and symbolize hope for human kind. Like the smell of acrid smoke, thoughts of Zephia's funeral take him from his reverie. Life on the island is tenuous for all persons. It is as unpredictable as a hurricane. The flutter of a butterfly's wing can have disastrous consequences for people thousands miles away.

Lee thinks about decisions made by men in authority, from generals to politicians. How many soldiers and civilians have died in vain? How many families have been disrupted? He turns and looks past Mr. Robert. The manse, in disrepair, rivets his attention. He gazes beyond it to see the barren cotton fields, not an acre in production. *What have we done?*